HALEY HAD SPENT THE LAST SEVERAL YEARS RUNNING AWAY. AWAY from James and his abuse. Away from job after job, failure after failure. Always afraid James would find them, again. She'd even failed her daughter. If she'd left James earlier, Trixie would never have witnessed the abuse. If she'd had more money, they wouldn't have lived in such a divey area of Seattle, Trixie wouldn't have witnessed the murder which stole her speech.

If, if, if. ...

Haley had screwed up so badly she had to run home again in order to save the two of them. Except that it wasn't home. It felt strange being here as an adult. Not how she would have imagined her life at this age.

Well, now she'd have to turn everything around. Help Trixie find her voice again. Make a success of her own life. Become a self-sufficient adult again.

CONTINENTAL DIVIDE

CONTINENTAL DIVIDE

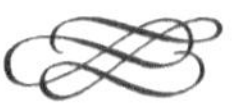

LINDA JORDAN

METAMORPHOSIS PRESS

Published by Metamorphosis Press

www.MetamorphosisPress.com

ISBN 13: 978-1946914033

For Michael & Zoe

CHAPTER 1 ~ HALEY

HALEY STEPPED OUT OF HER BLUE AND WHITE FJ CRUISER parked in the gravel driveway in front of Mom's ranch house. The house had been newly painted, or at least painted since Haley had been back home last. A cheery yellow with white trim. Mom probably liked it.

The sun was about to sink below the tree line, even though it wouldn't actually set for a couple more hours this time of year. The temperatures would begin to cool as soon as the sun disappeared behind the pines and spruces.

Haley stretched her stiff legs. She felt old, but forty wasn't old, was it? She tugged her too-tight jeans back into place and pulled the thin jacket around her.

She and her daughter, Trixie, had been on the road since three this morning. Why had she thought this was going to be a good idea? Her hands were shaking from too much coffee.

The pungent smell of pine trees filled her nose. The trees off to the right side of the yard had been limbed up and beneath them in permanent shade, lay patches of dirty snow. Out back a horse whinnied.

A black lab-shepherd mix came around the side of the

house, barked once and wagged its tail. The dog had a white chest. Maybe not a shepherd. Definitely a mix.

"Well, hi honey. What's your name?"

The dog came to her side and sat on top of her feet, waiting to be petted. It wore no collar or tag to give her an indication of its name. Haley stroked the dog's soft fur and the tail wagged even more.

Trixie still sat in the front seat, playing games on her phone. She hadn't even looked up when Haley parked.

"C'mon Trix. Put your phone away. Time to go in."

Trixie grimaced, but put her phone into the flowered backpack sitting at her feet. She grudgingly got out of the car. She was wearing jean cutoffs with fringed bottoms, running shoes and a ragged gray Psyduck t-shirt. Her shoulder-length brown hair was unruly and tangled.

Haley said, "Well, where's Mom, I wonder. Probably not in the house, but we'll try there first shall we?"

Trixie didn't answer

Haley knocked on the battered aluminum screen door. There was no answer.

She turned around to find Trixie on the wooden step right behind her, petting the dog.

"Let's go around back."

Haley gave a resigned sigh. She was finally here. It had been a long drive from Seattle. Returning home with her tail between her legs. A failed marriage, good riddance to him. Worse, was her failed tech career. At least she didn't have debt but there wasn't much money left either. She'd need to find work, fast.

They went around the left side of the house, onto the back patio. Mom was most likely out in one of the barns.

From the patio, a gravel area opened out onto the ranch itself. To the right of the house lay raised beds that used to hold Mom's fruit and vegetable garden. They probably weren't planted yet. All that was visible was bare soil. The beds were encased in a fence of wood and chicken wire with bird netting over the top to keep the deer and birds out. Behind the garden stood four small cabins built for guests, painted in sagebrush green and blue with white trim around the doors and windows. There were four other cabins, farther out on the property. Mom and Dad had all the cabins built about ten years ago. The house had six guest rooms, but some customers wanted a cabin all to themselves.

In the center stood a newly painted sagebrush green horse barn. It was tall and open inside with only a couple of wood stalls and a closed off heated tack room, plus a similarly secured feed room. The barn emptied out into a dirt paddock, which in turn led to a grass-filled pasture.

To the left of the horse barn was the hay barn. Separate from the horses, because Dad had once said he'd seen too many barn fires in his life and didn't want to see any more burned horses. It was after Dad died that Mom had opened the bed and breakfast business, even though she still raised cattle, too.

A wide gravel road led farther off to another wooden barn, this one painted a royal blue and shorter, used to house cattle when the weather got really bad.

They walked across the gravel road towards the horse barn. Out in the pasture twenty or so quarter horses, along with a few mixed breeds, grazed on new spring grass. The sky above was blue with no clouds and a dark shape passed slowly over them.

"Oh my god, look Trixie."

Trixie looked up, following the line of her finger.

"It's an eagle, I think a golden eagle."

Trixie looked at her, eyes open wide. Haley knew she'd never seen a bird that large.

"Yeah, their wingspans are wider than you are tall. Larger than bald eagles."

They stood as it circled above the pasture several times. Watching the large raptor brought her back to the land and how extraordinary it had felt growing up here, being part of nature and the elements.

At twelve, Trixie's age, she'd walked along the Blackfoot River, picking up stones that looked like jewels. Watched dragonflies hunt for prey. Become friends with frogs and toads.

That was before she grew up and got the urge to leave. The eagle finally rose a little higher and then passed beyond the tree line. Haley stood watching, hoping it would come back. When it didn't, they continued across the gravel.

They found Mom inside the open horse barn. She was sitting down, rubbing leather cleaner on a saddle.

"Hi Mom," Haley said.

"Haley. I wasn't expecting you this early."

Mom wiped her hands on a rag, got up and came towards her for a hug.

When had Mom gotten so small and shrunken?

"Well, and you must be Trixie."

Trixie nodded.

"Nice to meet you, dear. I'm your Grandmother. Bea. Short for Beatrix."

Mom hugged her. Then she hugged Trixie, who remained stiff, unwilling or unable to embrace a stranger. Mom either didn't notice or didn't call attention to it.

She said, "I see you've met Trouble."

"Trouble?" said Haley, looking down at the dog. "A self-fulfilling prophecy?"

"Oh no, we originally called her Raven, because her fur's so black and glossy. That was before she took a liking to hoarding."

"Hoarding?" asked Haley.

"Yeah, both her and the cat, Twinkletoes. They steal my guests' belongings. I think they're having a competition. Keep an eye on your things."

Haley laughed. "I think we saw a golden eagle over the pasture."

"They migrate through this time of year. Thousands of them. Amazing birds. That's why I built a chicken tractor, can't let my new hens run loose."

"Chicken tractors are all the rage in Seattle."

Her mom looked at her, surprised.

"But only with three chickens. I think that's the city limit. And no roosters."

Mom said, "Well, the world does change, doesn't it? Let's get you two settled in. I cleaned up a couple of rooms. They're not large. When I remodeled, the builders squeezed in an extra room by making them all a little smaller."

"The rooms will be fine, Mom."

The three of them walked back to her SUV, and Haley opened the tailgate. She pulled out a couple of battered suitcases. Trixie got her backpack from the front seat of the car and put it on. Then Trixie grabbed Haley's leather purse, handing it to her.

"Thanks dear," said Haley.

"You brought a lot of stuff," said Mom, cocking her head. Obviously not wanting to ask the question.

"Yeah, we moved out of our apartment," said Haley. "Not going back there."

"And this is all you own?" asked Mom.

"We sold or gave away everything else."

"Okay, then," said Mom. "Welcome home."

"We can unpack the rest of the stuff later," said Haley.

She shut the car up and locked it.

"You don't have to lock things here, you know."

"Habit," said Haley, picking up her suitcase and carrying it up the gravel driveway.

Trixie picked up her suitcase and followed them towards the house.

"I can help carry something. Where are my manners?" said Mom.

Trixie shook her head.

"We're used to carrying our own stuff," said Haley.

Mom opened the front door and said, "Mind the step up."

Haley walked inside and smelled fresh baked bread.

"I made up the blue room and the lilac room. Don't know who wants which one," said Mom, taking them through the spacious living room with its wood floors and yellow ochre walls. The furniture was old leather, a dark tan color. Green pillows and throws accented the room and tied in the large painting over the couch. A friend of Dad's had painted it when she was a kid. A scene of green pines and yellow leaved aspen trees, lining the edges of the Blackfoot River. *Fall on the Blackfoot* it was called.

They went down the hall towards the bedrooms, rolling their suitcases now.

Trixie went into the blue room and came back out nodding, then went back inside and closed the door. Haley took the lilac room. She looked around. A metal framed bed, painted white with a white and lilac flowered bedspread. The walls were a perfect shade of lavender. A lilac dresser sat next to the closet. In a corner, between two floral curtained windows that looked out into the pine forest sat a lilac painted table and chair.

A place for her laptop. And for herself to pull her life back together again.

"This is perfect Mom."

"Good. It's one of my favorite rooms."

"Do you have guests scheduled soon?"

"A couple are coming this weekend. More next week. Our busy season is on its way. We're never full up though. Not since the economy tanked."

"Things are picking up though, at least in the Seattle area."

"Not around here. Winnie's cafe is empty far too often for breakfast and lunch. No tourists are coming through. People are taking the new highway over by Helena. They're in a hurry.

Or if they come through, they don't stop. Have you had dinner?"

"We had a burger in Missoula."

"That was hours ago. I made a casserole. I'll go see what else I can find. I'll let you unpack," Mom said. Then she checked to make sure Trixie wasn't in earshot, and whispered, "She's still not speaking?"

"No. I don't expect her to anytime soon. It's been years. I just let it go. I don't want to pressure her. When she has something to say, she'll let us know."

Mom shook her head and said, "Poor girl." Then left for the kitchen.

Haley looked down the hall. Trixie's door was closed, but she could hear the sound of drawers opening.

Haley unpacked her suitcase, full of cheap thrift store clothes she didn't like, but at least they fit. Then stuck the suitcase in the back of the closet. She went out to the car and brought in her computer. She plugged in a surge protector and the computer. Mom didn't have internet or a computer.

Haley would have to make a few calls, see what internet options were available. Probably only satellite. Lincoln was a town living in the past. She intended to change some of that.

If no one was going to pay her to use her skills back in Seattle, then she'd live here and work for free. She'd just have to figure out what would help people the most.

Haley couldn't help the person who needed help the most. Trixie was the only one who could help herself. All Haley could do was love her and keep her safe.

CHAPTER 2 ~ MABEL

MABEL STOOD IN HER ROSE PINK BATHROOM AND LOOKED AT her silver hair in the mirror. She should wear a wig. That would help. She dug into a cabinet drawer and found the old brown wig she'd worn back in the sixties, when wigs were common. She shook it out and pulled it onto her head, tucking her short hair beneath it.

Perfect. Absolutely perfect.

She took it off and left the bathroom, switching off the light.

Out in her cozy little kitchen she put the wig in her purse, placing it on top of Mac's old pistol and snapped the clasp shut. She filled a bottle of water, setting it on the counter by her purse.

Everything was ready for her little trip. Her house was clean and tidy, everything in its place. Lights were turned off. The license plates of Mac's car had been smeared with mud so as to make them illegible. The snow tires were still on because there was still snow in places.

It was a good thing she hadn't gotten rid of all his cars when he died all those years ago. She'd just never gotten around to it.

They'd come in handy now. All that car insurance she'd paid over the years like a good citizen should. She'd only kept one car licensed, but it was a simple thing to move the plates around. The stupid cars were about to pay for themselves.

She picked up her purse and bottle and left the house. The streets had been plowed, so most of the snow was gone, but a layer of black ice lay on the road. She'd paid the neighbor kid, Jameson, to shovel her walks and driveway, but there was still ice out there too.

Mabel locked the back door and held onto the iron rail as she went down the slippery, concrete stair. Then she took small steps across the ice to the garage.

Once inside, she pushed the button of the remote control to open the large garage door behind the big Ford 4-wheel drive pickup. The roads were sort of dicey out today. She'd be happy when all the ice was melted and gone.

Even though this was just a dry run, she wanted to be prepared. The pickup was brown with a tan panel down the side, so it would blend in well. The truck looked just like half a dozen other pickups she saw every day.

She set her belongings in the passenger's side, closed the door and walked slowly around to the driver's side to get in. It took a lot of effort to haul herself up into it. She'd better get to work using that treadmill and lifting those weights. This might be a little harder than she thought.

She'd have to be able to move fast. Some idiot might get it into their head to chase her.

Once inside, she took a few deep breaths. She could do this. She started up the truck. This was going to be fun.

At the crossroads, she took 141 south to Helena. She'd poke around the small towns on the way there and choose one that looked likely.

She finally found one. It was a small town. Like her home, Lincoln, but a little larger. One main road running straight through town. She stopped at an old gas station, one with no security cameras, and pumped her own gas breathing in the gas fumes. She'd always liked the smell of gasoline.

Mabel paid in cash. Then pulled around to the side of the station, slipped her wig on and tied an old see through peach colored scarf over the top of it. Now she looked like a proper old lady.

Not that anyone would notice. No one ever did notice old ladies.

She drove down the street to the drug store. The sign read *Barney's Drugstore.*

She glanced at the clock on her dashboard. 2:50. Good. Schools were still in session. No kids hanging around. She parallel parked in front, making sure there was a lot of space in front of her.

The pickup wasn't visible from the store windows, but was close enough to the door. The streets were empty.

Mabel supposed she should have had a getaway driver. But no one else needed to be involved in this. No one else needed to know. And who else would be desperate enough to do this?

Inside the store, Mabel looked around.

It was small, crowded with too many shelves. The store smelled sweet, all that candy. No security cameras.

She felt nervous.

Just one employee on the floor. A middle-aged man who'd had too many good meals, too much stress and too little exercise. Must be Barney.

No one else was in the store.

'I'm invisible,' she told herself silently.

This was it.

Mabel walked up to the counter and unsnapped her handbag. She pulled the pistol out.

"Put all your money in a bag and hand it over."

"What?" said the man, looking up from his cellphone.

"Put all the money in a bag and hand it over!" she said, louder. "And don't push any alarm buttons."

The man stood up quickly when she waved the gun at him.

He opened the cash register. Filled the bag.

"Everything under the drawer too," she said.

He lifted the cash drawer. Pulled out a few hundreds. Put those in the bag.

"You want checks?" he asked, his voice breaking.

"No. Hand it over. Give me your cell phone. Then get on the floor. I'll leave your phone outside on the sidewalk. Wait at least until ten minutes have passed before you move. Don't call anyone."

He gave her the phone. Then scrambled onto the floor.

She turned and ran out. Her legs felt wobbly.

She set his phone on a window ledge, outside the door. Ran for the pickup. Hauled herself up inside. Started it and drove like a bat out of hell. Towards Helena.

As she drove, Mabel caught her breath. She stashed the gun back in her purse and pulled the scarf and wig off. The bag of money went under her seat. She hoped it would be enough.

As she roared down the road, at the speed limit of course, her hands shook on the steering wheel. She could smell the old pine tree air freshener hanging from the mirror, its scent enlivened by the heat pouring out of the vents.

She pulled over in Helena and stopped at an old burger place. She took the cash, counted it, organizing it into 100's, 20's, 10's, etc. and put it in her wallet. Then she got out of the pickup and put the paper bag in an outside garbage can.

She got back in the pickup and drove off. She picked up Highway 279 and drove carefully on the icy roads over the pass. Mabel nibbled on some beef jerky that had been in her purse, while driving. She was starving. Should've bought a burger at that place.

This was supposed to be just a dry run. To check out the

drugstore. But it seemed like a chance worth taking at the time. Mabel still couldn't believe she'd done it.

She ran into Highway 200 and turned West, towards Lincoln.

Her hands had long stopped shaking.

The money amounted to $3,498.89. She could make that last for quite a few months. Along with social security.

Yes indeedy, invisibility was her superpower.

CHAPTER 3 ~ HALEY

THE NEXT MORNING HALEY WOKE WHEN THE SUN STREAMED through the thin curtains. Her phone said it was not long after five.

Haley rolled over and tried to go back to sleep, but it was too light. She heard the sounds of Mom puttering around in the kitchen, making breakfast. Even through the closed door, Haley could smell coffee. And bacon.

That did it. She got up and pulled on a pair of well worn jeans and a blue t-shirt. She topped that with a flannel shirt, then put on thin socks and a pair of black dressy boots, the only ones she had. Made for going out on the town, not for scuffing around the ranch.

She'd need to go into town and get a pair of riding boots. Trixie would need some too. At twelve, her feet were still growing rapidly, along with the rest of her body. She probably needed all new clothes. Well for now, boots would have to do.

Haley went down the hall to the bathroom and splashed water on her face. After drying it, she went back to her room and brushed her hair. Her face felt dry and scaly. She hadn't even been here a day and the lack of humidity was already taking its toll. Moisturizer it was. After that she went back down the hall to the kitchen.

"Good morning, Mom."

"Good morning. Haley this is Jerry and Dani," said Mom, nodding to the two people at the table, drinking coffee. "This is Haley, my daughter. Her daughter, Trixie, came with her. She doesn't talk. You'll see both of them around."

"Hello," said Haley.

"I'm Jerry," said the tall, gangly, fiftyish man, standing and holding out his hand. "Pleased to meet you ma'am."

"Please, just call me Haley. Ma'am makes me feel old." She shook his hand. The skin felt dry and scratchy, from cuts and callouses.

The young woman, probably in her twenties said, "I'm Dani." She held out her hand next.

Haley shook it and then sat down at the old wooden table, grabbing the coffeepot and filling her mug.

"Jerry and Dani have cabins over past the horse pasture. Since Glen, ..." Mom paused as if to make herself redo something, "your father died, we've been meeting here in the morning to figure out the day's work. I so often need to be around to get breakfast for the guests. It just works out better than what your father used to do."

Was Mom trying to stop saying Dad's name? Why was that?

"The coffee's better too," said Jerry.

Haley smiled and grabbed a slice of bacon. She watched Mom pour batter into a cast iron skillet for pancakes.

The bacon crunched pleasantly in her mouth, the smoky taste released. Haley closed her eyes, enjoying it. When was the last time she'd had bacon? When was the last time she'd actually cooked? Not just heated up something instant. She couldn't remember.

"Will Trixie be joining us?" asked Mom.

"Probably not for hours. She's almost a teenager. She needs

ten to twelve hours of sleep. And yesterday I made her get up at two in the morning to drive so we could get an early start."

"Whyever did you want to leave so early?"

"I wasn't sure if we'd stop in Spokane or Missoula or just drive straight through. I wanted it to be light whenever it was we stopped driving. It seemed like a good idea at the time." Haley didn't explain the real reason she'd wanted to leave so early.

"Well, you're here safe and sound. That's what counts. I'm going into town today. I need to get groceries for the weekend. Do you two want to come?"

"Yes. We both need to get some boots. And I'd like to see Winnie."

"Okay. How about ten?"

"That works for us. Trixie should have had enough sleep by then," Haley said, smiling.

Mom acted as if she was planning an expedition. Into town was only a couple miles away. In Seattle that wasn't even across town. This was another world. Lincoln was tiny, just over a thousand people.

Mom, Jerry and Dani went over things that needed to happen during the day. Checking out a horse's hoof, moving the cattle to a different pasture, fixing a broken fencepost in the pasture the cattle were currently in, fixing wiring in one of the cabins where mice had gotten in and chewed the wiring through over the winter. Then the two workers finished off their coffee, put their mugs in the sink, said goodbye and went out the back door.

Haley ate pancakes when Mom brought them to the table. Spreading peanut butter on them, then syrup.

Mom finally sat down to eat and stared at her.

"What?" asked Haley.

"I'd forgotten you used to do that. So did your father." Mom's face wrinkled up.

"Mom, I'm sorry."

"No, it's okay. It just takes time. I still miss him."

"It's only been a few months. Of course you miss him. At least you've had some company, so you're not all alone."

"Well, other than those two, there's been a few guests, but not many. And there's Winnie, but she's always at the cafe. I've been having coffee with Mabel sometimes."

"Who's Mabel?"

"Mabel McTavish, your old kindergarten teacher."

"Mrs. McTavish?"

Mom nodded. "She's retired now. Her husband died many years ago. Cancer, probably from Vietnam. All that Agent Orange. She's having a hard time of it, poor gal. Social security and medicare don't stretch very far and the government has refused to help pay most of the medical bills. All that red tape. But she says there's a windfall coming soon. Some inheritance or something. She's not sure when."

Haley nodded.

There was a mrrowing at the back door. Mom got up and opened it. In walked a huge gray and white cat dragging a tan leather glove.

"Twink, you've done it again." Mom snatched the glove away and went back outside where she pinned it to a clothesline that hung beneath the roof covering the stone patio.

Haley noticed the clothesline held jewelry, several other gloves, a scarf, a magazine and a red sock.

The cat, whose fur had to be two inches long, rubbed against Haley's legs. She petted him and he purred loudly. Very proud of his catch.

"Such a bad cat," said Mom. "He steals anything he can. I just pin stuff up there for people to retrieve." Mom reached down and picked him up to cuddle him, clearly he wasn't that bad of a cat. Haley could hear his purr from across the room.

Mom came back and sat down at the table.

"I need to have an internet connection," said Haley. "If I get one hooked up, then your guests can use it. They'll like that."

"Then I'll pay for it," said Mom.

"It's okay. I can cover it."

"But if my guests are using it, then I should. And I can take it off the taxes, as a business expense," she said, proudly. "I just don't understand the interwebs yet or know how to go about it. I still don't have a computer, you know."

"I know. But if you did, you could set things up to take reservations automatically. You wouldn't have to worry about missed phone calls."

"That would be complicated, what with choosing between cabins and rooms."

"I could build you a website which explained the choices."

"Well, if you can make it work, that would be nice. I think. It gets a lot to handle sometimes. Reservations, along with cooking and laundry. You wouldn't believe the laundry. I'm always washing bedding. I have a woman come in to help clean. I just can't keep up. Jerry and Dani do most of the ranch stuff, but I still have to keep tabs on everything."

"Of course you can't keep up, you're doing the work that both you and Dad used to do."

"You're right. That's why I hired Dani. So Jerry could take over some of Glen's work. But I still need to oversee everything," she said, firmly.

"I can help, if you want. I don't know what you need help with, but I can clean and do laundry. And build the website, take over reservations. I can work in the kitchen, clean and chop. I'm not a great cook, you know that."

"Well, that would help a lot, thank you. I don't want you to have to work for a place to stay though. You know you're welcome to stay here as long as you need. Permanently, if that's what you'd like. It's so nice to finally see Trixie. She's a lovely young girl."

"Yes, she is. I'm sorry it took so long for us to get out here. First it was James, then after that ended, we just didn't have the money, or I couldn't take the time away from work without risking losing my job."

"But you did lose it, didn't you?" asked Mom, a sad note in her voice.

"I lost several. One company collapsed just after another. I rode out the demise of five tech companies. After that, there were just no more jobs. I was working in restaurants, waiting tables to make ends meet and they still weren't meeting. Seattle's too expensive. After Dad died, I finally decided to pack up and leave Seattle before we burned through all our savings. I've been homeschooling Trixie, she hated all her schools. She was way ahead in all her classes and there's only a month left in the school year, so I arranged for her to take the year end tests so in the fall she can move up to the next grade. Then we packed up and left. I'm so glad to be back in the sunshine," she said, looking out the kitchen window, not yet willing to tell Mom the whole story. Not yet. Maybe never.

"Well, we've got sun, that's for sure."

Haley spent the next couple of hours using Mom's phone book and her own cell phone, trying to find the best satellite company. She finally arranged for an appointment on Friday. Two more days without internet. The withdrawal was awful. She used up almost all her data allowance for the month.

At nine, Trixie wandered out of her bedroom. She came and knocked on Haley's open door.

"Good morning sweetheart. Did you sleep well."

Trixie nodded, she looked groggy. Her hair was all mussed up and she still wore her pajamas, a mismatched pair of blue sleep pants and a black t-shirt with a sparkly unicorn on it.

"Grandma's left breakfast on the table. She's outside. Eat some breakfast and get dressed. At ten we're going into town."

Trixie scrunched up her face.

"I know. The last thing I want to do is get into a car. But we both need some boots and town is just five minutes away."

Trixie nodded and wandered out towards the kitchen.

Haley added up the money they'd spent yesterday for gas and meals. She had enough cash left for a couple pairs of boots. After that, she'd have to take money out of the tiny savings account.

She tossed all her scribblings about the various satellite companies and their rates into the garbage can beneath the table. Then went back to her room and put the budget stuff away in a desk drawer, got her coat and closed the lavender door.

Trixie had left her door open, so Haley peeked in to make sure the cat wasn't inside and closed it as well. Out in the kitchen, Trixie sat at the table eating pancakes. Twinkletoes sat on the chair next to her, completely mesmerized and purring up a storm.

"How do you like Twink?" asked Haley.

Trixie smiled.

Haley poured some milk for Trixie and set it in front of her.

"I thought I'd go for a walk, before we go to town, want to come?"

Trixie nodded.

"Get a move on then."

Trixie finished up her pancakes and milk, while nuzzling Twinkletoes, who was lapping up the affection. Haley grabbed a strip of bacon and poured another mug of coffee. The coffee didn't taste as rich as her own, the beans she used were better, but it was good. Better than Mom used to make when Haley was younger. That awful pre-ground stuff from the can.

Trixie went into her room and came back dressed in jeans, plain blue t-shirt and old running shoes, faster than Haley would have thought possible.

"Get a coat," she said.

Trixie motioned at the sun through the window.

"Yeah, it's sunny here, but it's only forty five degrees outside. It's cold."

Trixie grudgingly went back to her room. She returned wearing a black Smaug hoody.

Haley sighed, and put on her warm coat and gloves. She pulled a knit hat over her head and they went out the back door. Twinkletoes followed them.

It was brisk outside and the sky was totally clear, no clouds. The horses were up near the barn, eating hay from the open center of a couple huge tractor tires that Dad had long ago laid on the ground and converted to feeders. The corral was bordered by wood posts and a three rail fence. Just like when she'd been a kid. It had been easy to squeeze between the horizontal rails to get into the corral.

There were at least twenty horses out in the paddock. Haley didn't recognize any of them, but she hadn't been home in what, fifteen years? These looked mostly like Quarter Horses. Good for working cattle and taking guests on trail rides. Mostly bays, sorrels and blacks, but there was a white one, a palomino and a couple of pintos. And one Appaloosa. There were a couple of just born foals, both chocolate brown with flaxen manes and tails. Which was strange. She just saw mares and geldings. Mom would have kept a stallion separate, though.

Mom came out of the barn, waved at them and came over.

"Good morning Trixie."

Trixie waved.

"Mom, do you have a stallion hidden somewhere?"

"Oh no," she laughed. "Sam, who owns the old Linden place, wants to breed horses. Some fancy new breed, Rocky Mountain Horses. They're called gaited horses, an extra gait that makes for smooth riding, he says. Anyway, he got this young stud before he bought any mares. The poor guy got lonely and managed to open three gates and came down here to visit a couple of my mares, who happened to be in heat. So, I got a couple bonuses."

Haley laughed. "Did he charge you a stud fee?"

Mom looked at her and said, "Naw. Told him he was lucky I didn't castrate the horse. Opened one of our gates and some of the horses were out on the highway. But nobody was hurt and we got them all back safely. Smart bugger that one."

"Cute little foals," Haley said.

"Yes, they're adorable. Look just like their dad. I hope they prove to be smooth riding. I wasn't up for training a couple young ones, but it needs to happen."

"Well, you've got us to help out around the house now," Haley said.

She looked at Trixie who was fascinated by the horses. Growing up in Seattle, Trixie had rarely seen them. Whenever they'd seen police horses, she'd always wanted to go pet them. Sometimes that happened. When the horse and officer weren't actively working.

One of the bay geldings came up to the fence.

"This is Spitz."

"Spitz?" asked Haley.

"Dad named him. He had a different name, but then we found he likes to swim. If you want to go in the river, he's the horse to take. We finally got a waterproof saddle, just for him."

Trixie was stroking the horse's muzzle. He moved closer and stood, closing his eyes.

"Well, looks like you've got him wrapped around your little finger," said Mom.

Trixie smiled and kept petting the horse.

"I'll go and clean up. Then we can go," said Mom.

"Okay, yell when you're ready," said Haley.

Haley could tell Trixie was happy being around so many animals. They'd never had pets. Having to move so often to run away from James, every time he tracked them down, meant needing to find new apartments quickly. Not easy to find cheap rentals that accepted pets. A twinge of guilt flashed through Haley. She'd made so many bad choices that hurt her daughter's life.

"Would you like to learn how to take care of the horses and ride?" she asked.

Trixie's eyes widened. She smiled and nodded enthusiastically.

"Okay, then we'll make it happen."

They hung out and petted any horse who came over to the fence until Mom was ready.

Then piled into Mom's cherry red, four-wheel drive pickup and drove to town. The two lane highway was lined with pines and still bare aspen trees, their white bark gleaming in the sunlight. Just before town, the trees diminished, the landscape opened up into grass and sagebrush. Even with the windows closed she could smell the pungent sage.

Lincoln hadn't changed much. There were a couple new businesses at this end of town. New colors of paint and a few facelifts of older buildings. She could see a few more changes farther down the road. This was the old highway that ran straight through town, so it was a wide road with lots of pullover space. All the parking lots were gravel and there weren't any barriers between lots. Truckers and buses needed the space to pull over and park.

Mom pulled up in front of the grocery store, an old concrete block building painted sea green.

"Where shall we go first?" asked Mom.

"How about boots first? Then Winnie's. Then groceries," said Haley.

"Sounds like a plan."

They got out and walked two buildings down to the mercantile store, Johnson's. It had few display windows in front and was painted a brownish red. The store sold clothes, kitchen goods, farm supplies and a lot of toys and touristy items. And boots.

Mom walked in and said, "Hello Sheila, how are you this morning?"

"Well, Bea, nice to see you. I'm feeling fine, and you," said the kind-faced elderly woman behind the counter.

"I'm doing well. I've got my girls with me, you remember Haley and this is her daughter Trixie."

"Well, Haley! I haven't seen you in so long. And Trixie, nice to meet you."

"Hi," said Haley, vaguely recognizing the woman.

Trixie smiled. It had been a very long time since Trixie smiled at a stranger.

"We've come to get some boots," said Mom.

"Do you want to look first, or do you want my help now?"

"We'll look first," said Haley.

"Okay, just yell when you're ready," said Sheila.

They walked back to the boots. It took her all of a minute to choose a style for herself. Plain golden brown leather with square toes and plenty of room. She found the right size and tried them on. The stiff leather smelled lovely. They fit perfectly, but would feel better once they were broken in. And the price was right. She put her cheap old fashion boots back on and remained sitting.

Trixie wandered back and forth, trying to decide.

"Let me know when you find something you want to try on, honey," Haley said.

Trixie finally held up a pair of fancy turquoise boots with cutouts of lacy leaves in brown leather, her face questioning.

Normally Trixie never wore anything except black. Haley had been sure Trixie would pick a pair of black boots. Haley stood up and looked at the boots.

"Beautiful boots. They'll get dirty quickly, you know that?"

Trixie nodded. Haley looked at the bottom of the boot and blanched.

"Expensive little puppies."

Trixie nodded, her face drooping. Haley noticed she didn't go back to looking at other boots. Maybe they'd splurge.

"Okay find the right size and try them on."

Trixie smiled and put the sample boot back on the shelf and began looking through the boxes below for her size.

"Well, that was fast," said Mom. She glanced at her watch. "I think I'll go over to Winnie's and make sure we can get a table."

"Okay. We'll meet you over there."

"Here's the keys, you can put your boots in the truck and then lock it. Town is different from the ranch." Mom went off towards the front of the store.

Trixie tried on two pairs before she found the right fit. She was grinning so widely by the time she had both boots on, Haley had a hard time not laughing. They should have moved out here years ago. Even if Dad was still alive.

"Do you want to wear them?" asked Haley.

Trixie nodded and put her running shoes in the boot box, closing it.

They went to the front of the store to pay.

Sheila took their boxes and rang up the prices, then handed the boxes back, along with the receipt. Then she moved on to writing something on a pad and said, "You girls have a fun day."

"Here's the money," said Haley, handing it to her.

"Oh honey, I can't take your money. Bea said to put it on her tab. We bill her by the month."

Haley's mouth dropped open. She hadn't expected that and couldn't figure out if she felt relieved, guilty or annoyed.

"Well, thank you," said Haley, politely.

"Any time. And welcome home."

CHAPTER 4 ~ MABEL

Mabel sat at the wooden kitchen table, drinking a cup of sweet cocoa out of her favorite mug. She ran her fingers over the embossed red letters which read *You can't scare me. I'm a teacher*. She'd painted her nails a bright red which matched the writing. She hadn't used nail polish in about thirty years and had forgotten how smelly it was.

The tv news was on, a Helena station. It made a brief mention of the robbery. Calling her the *Granny Bandit*. It was in the feel good section of the news. There were no photos, just an interview with the owner, Barney.

He didn't give a good description of her. At least not in the interview. And the police drawing looked nothing like her. That was all good. She'd stick close to home and not do anything out of the ordinary for quite a while. Except maybe paint her nails.

She had friends to see. Blankets to crochet for babies. Potlucks to go to. There was more than enough here to keep her busy. And now she had enough money tucked away in the linen closet to keep her in groceries and medicine for quite a while.

To hell with the government and their nonpayment on

Mac's medical bills. They'd sent him over to Vietnam with hundreds of other young men, then poisoned them all with agent orange. The resulting cancers and other medical issues should have been paid for. His death, they could never pay her back for that. The cancer and other problems had come and gone several times since he'd hit forty. Then he'd finally died of it at sixty. It had taken her ten years, after his death, to pay the medical bills. Their savings was gone and she couldn't live on what social security sent her way.

So, short of declaring bankruptcy, a life of crime was her way out. She'd given it a lot of thought. She'd only rob places when she had to. And not hurt anyone. And steal from businesses who would be covered by insurance. She would have liked to hit those newish drugstores or banks, but their security was too good. Mabel regretted stealing from Mom and Pop stores.

So, she'd just have to do it as little as possible and be frugal with her money. She was good at that.

Mabel stirred the cocoa to mix up the stuff at the bottom of the cup and sipped the chocolately liquid. Then smiled. It was going to be great fun having a superpower.

And nobody would ever think of her as a thief. Not her, a retired elementary school teacher, who taught all her kids how to be well behaved. For decades. Mabel had always followed the rules.

Well, she was done with that.

CHAPTER 5 ~ HALEY

HALEY AND TRIXIE PUT THEIR BOOT BOXES IN THE PICKUP and walked over to Winnie's. The little cafe had had a facelift since Haley had seen it last. The wood building was painted an attractive purple orchid color with scarlet trim, which made it look like a place one wanted to eat. A wooden hitching post still separated the gravel parking lot from the paved sidewalk. She'd never seen the hitching post in use, but none of the cars were parked in front of it either. A couple of semis had pulled over next to the highway and parked.

The cafe had two large picture windows and a glass door. The place looked pretty full for lunchtime on a Wednesday.

They went inside and looked around for Mom. There was a counter with swiveling metal and upholstered stools, only two seats open. The ten tables in the front room were full. The smells of strong coffee brewing and burgers cooking permeated the air.

They found Mom at a table in the back room, chatting with Winnie. Winnie was dressed in jeans, sneakers and a purple shirt. Her long gray hair was tied up in a pony tail.

The back room had fewer windows so it was a little dark.

There were a couple open tables, but most of the twelve tables were occupied. Winnie's must have a good reputation. Haley and Trixie sat down in straight back wood chairs.

"Oh hello Haley," said Winnie, giving her a hug. "And this must be Trixie. My you're almost full grown. Oh, I love your boots."

"We just bought them, at Johnson's," said Haley.

Winnie winked and said, "Nothing like a good pair of boots to bring out the wildness in a woman. Well, here's some menus and our specials are on the board there. I made coconut meringue pies this morning. I remember you used to love them, Haley."

"You've got an amazing memory," said Haley, surprised.

"I do try. Well, I'll let you read the menu and I'll be back." Winnie whisked off into the front room. Haley hoped she had that much energy at sixty.

It didn't take long to decide on food. Mom chose the clam chowder. No one made egg salad like Winnie's, so Haley chose that. Trixie chose a B.A.L.T. Winnie's had kept pace with the times. When Haley was a kid, Winnie hadn't had access to exotic vegetables like avocados.

Winnie did the baking, starting around four in the morning and her husband, Eddy, staffed the kitchen from six in the morning until three in the afternoon. After finishing the baking, Winnie mainly waited tables, along with hired help, and did customer relations. Haley saw at least one other server besides Winnie. Perhaps, they had more. At three the cafe closed for the day. Winnie's baked goods were always much in demand. Haley's mouth was watering for some of that pie.

"Those really are the cutest boots," Mom said to Trixie.

Trixie straightened her legs, showing off her boots and smiling.

"Mom, you didn't have to pay for our boots," said Haley. "We have a little money."

"I know honey, but I've got more money than you right now. And I've never had the opportunity to spoil my granddaughter. Plus it's been a very long time since I've been able to spoil you, either. And it looks like you could use some spoiling."

"Well, thank you," said Haley. "We appreciate the gifts. It looks like Winnie's doing pretty well here."

"They're having a good day. But there aren't enough of them."

"Is it really bad?"

"They're not planning on closing, but they could use some help."

"I'll talk to her and see what I can do."

"I'm sure she'd be grateful for any help."

An elderly woman came up to the table. She wore thick glasses and had curly short, silver white hair. Even with the bold, cherry colored pantsuit and white walking shoes, she looked frail.

"Mabel, you remember Haley, and this is her daughter Trixie."

"How could I forget Haley? It's wonderful to see you, dear. And to meet your daughter." Mrs. McTavish smiled at Trixie, who politely returned the smile.

"Mrs. McTavish. What a nice surprise."

"Please, call me Mabel. I'm retired."

"Mabel."

"I came over to pick up a piece of pie for dinner, just thought I'd come say hello. Are we still meeting for coffee day after tomorrow?" she asked Mom.

"I'll be here," said Mom."

"Mabel nodded and said, "Lovely to see you again Haley. And nice to meet you Trixie."

Haley nodded and Trixie waved.

Then Mabel turned and made her way back to the front room.

"She's such a dear," said Mom. "Never a bad word to say about anyone."

The food came and Haley devoured her egg salad sandwich, savoring the rich melange of flavors: egg, salt and real mayonnaise. The taste was cut by mustard and rounded out with the soft whole wheat bread, made by Winnie. When she finished, Haley felt satisfied and content.

"Mom, what are your plans for the ranch?"

"I haven't given it a lot of thought."

"But if you could make it whatever you wanted, if you could have your life be whatever you wanted, what would that be?"

"I'd like a vacation."

"Where?"

"I think I'd like to go somewhere warm and lie on a beach or near a pool. Drink exotic tropical drinks with umbrellas. With a friend, of course."

"Who?"

"Winnie would be nice."

"Okay, for how long?"

"A couple of weeks would do it. I couldn't lie around for much longer than that, I think."

"So what's preventing you from doing that, say in the middle of winter?"

"Money, the ranch."

"But can't Jerry and Dani handle the ranch?"

"I just hired Dani, after your father died. I suppose they could, but there's not enough money. Everything we make gets poured back into the ranch."

"If you had more paying guests, would that make things work financially?"

"I think it would. If we were mostly full from mid-May through the end of September, that would do it. Along with the cattle sales, which isn't that much, but it brings in a little."

"I've been thinking, besides making you a website, which

would be advertising and also take reservations, what else can we offer to guests? Free wi-fi will be good, but perhaps you could offer a few other amenities."

"Like what?"

"Some sort of entertainment. You've got trail rides. And Jerry takes people fishing, right?"

Mom nodded.

"Well, what do people do in the evening?"

Sit around and read, mostly. Some watch tv, in the tv room. But there's never much on."

"Well, isn't there stuff to do outside?"

"Mosquitos."

"Okay, let's deal with that. How about if we put in a hot tub and a sauna? Inside an enclosure so people wouldn't get eaten by mosquitos. Maybe find some local musicians to come out on the weekends? A barn dance once every couple of weeks?"

"Interesting," said Mom.

"Maybe have someone local who's a massage therapist available for reservations."

"These are good ideas, but they all take extra work."

"Yes, they do. I'm here to do some of the work. We should keep thinking of ideas. Things that would fit into this part of the country and would make tourists happy. Then after we have a long list, we can toss out the ideas we don't want to try."

"That sounds like a good plan."

The crowd in the cafe was beginning to thin out and another server had taken over Winnie's job. Winnie brought their desserts and pulled up another chair, plopping down in it.

"Well, what're you all talking about? You all look fascinated."

"We're thinking up ideas on how to make the ranch better," said Mom. "Haley makes websites. She thinks that'll help us a lot. She also thinks she should make one for your cafe too."

"I've been thinkin' about getting one. I don't even advertise in the papers. I know I should, but it all takes time I'd rather spend baking."

"Word of mouth is the best advertising," said Haley, "but first you've got to get more people in here. Then you've got to keep them happy. If more people came do you have the staff and food to serve them?"

"We'd have to hire a couple more people, but there's always young people looking for work. Especially in the summer."

"Well then, let me see what I can come up with."

"How much would you charge?" asked Winnie.

"I think I'd be happy to be paid in pie," said Haley, the coconut meringue taste lingering in her mouth. The texture of the fluffy meringue, the fluffy coconut pudding and flaky butter crust were perfection. The pie filled her with a sense of well being. Not like anyone else's dessert. Winnie's desserts went beyond that. This was nirvana.

"Funny you. But you can't live off of pie."

"Right now, I'm okay. Mom's not charging us rent. I will need money eventually, but for now, I'm doing well. If you like the website and it's working, then you can pay me by word of mouth."

"Well, I do have a bulletin board. With slots for business cards. Over there on the wall." Winnie pointed to a large cork board covered with ads and notices. Alongside it was a clear plastic piece with little holders for business cards."

"I guess I better make up some business cards," said Haley. This was going to be fun.

"How's the river doing out at your place?" asked Winnie.

"It's running pretty high, already. And the snow's just beginning to melt," said Mom, shaking her head.

"I've heard the weather's going to be warm in the next few weeks. They're expecting flooding."

"I guess we'll be flooded again."

"How much of the property?" asked Haley.

"Most of the River Pasture. That's why we have so few cows right now. We sold off so many last fall. Just can't sustain them any more, not in the spring when their pasture's under water."

Haley hadn't been out to the River Pasture or anywhere near the Blackfoot River since she'd last visited over twenty years ago. But it didn't flood that often. In the spring it always ran high from snow melt, then dwindled in the late summer to a reasonable river you could wade in. Even swim in the deeper parts.

Mom turned to her, "The river changed its course a few years ago when it flooded. It's never gone back to the old one. It's cut quite a ways into our land. We lost an acre or two. Gained about the same farther upstream, but that's all sand and gravel, old river bed. Won't keep the cows fed. We need to redo the fence before we open up those flooded pastures every year now. More work."

Haley nodded.

A tall man, with dark shoulder-length hair and stubble on his face, came over to the table. He was dressed in jeans, a blue flannel shirt and a down coat. He looked about her age.

"Hello Winnie, Bea," he said, looking at Mom and Winnie.

"Well Sam, nice to see you," said Mom.

"Hi Sam, have you got your piece of pie yet?" asked Winnie.

"Not yet."

"I'll have Martha set one aside for you. Otherwise, it'll be gone soon." She waved the waitress over and gave her instructions.

"Thank you. Can't miss my pie, Winnie. Otherwise, the day's just ruined." He brushed the hair back from his startling blue eyes.

"Pull up a chair, Sam," said Mom.

"I don't want to interrupt you."

"No interruption. Sam, this is my daughter Haley and her

daughter Trixie. They've come to stay with me. Permanently, if I can convince them."

"Nice to meet you," he said. "How are those two foals doing?"

"They're doing well. The spitting image of their daddy," said Mom.

"I sure am sorry about that. When the time comes send them over to my place and I'll get them started right."

"That's really not necessary," said Mom.

"It's the least I could do. I know you weren't expecting a couple of little ones to be sprung on you. They'll make excellent riding horses for your guests in a few years. If you'd like I can come over and get them used to a halter and being led around. It's never too early to work with them just a little. I know you're short of time."

"You better take him up on it, Bea. People pay hundreds of dollars to have him show them how to work with their horses," said Winnie.

"I've only done a few clinics," said Sam, looking down. "Mostly, I just work with my own horses."

"And sell them for large amounts of money," said Winnie.

"Well, I've gotta pay for that pie somehow."

Sam seemed very interesting. Haley couldn't stop looking at him, listening to his quiet, calm voice.

"Sam, sit down," said Winnie, pulling up an empty chair. "Do you have a website?"

He sat down on the chair Winnie got for him. He looked uncomfortable. The type of guy more comfortable alone or with animals, than with other people. Not the kind of guy she was usually attracted to.

And yet...

Sam said, "Yeah, I had a guy make me one, but I don't know how to change anything on it and it's sort of a mess, and he's disappeared. I have better photos of the horses, and the ranch, that I'd like to put on it. And I want to list the horses I have currently for sale."

"Haley makes websites. She's going to make one for Bea and one for the cafe. Maybe you need to hire her too."

"Well, if you've got an opening in your schedule, I could really use some help," he said, smiling, charmingly.

"I wouldn't have to travel far," she said.

He was flirting with her. So the shy thing must be just an act. Well, she wasn't in the market. Hadn't been for years. Would she ever be interested enough in a man to date again?

"Nope, I'm just a stone's throw away. You should come over, both of you," he said, including Trixie in his gaze. "And meet the horses. You can see those two little foals' daddy. He thinks he's something else."

"You don't think he is?" asked Haley.

"I think he will be. He's young yet and has a lot to learn."

"What are you training him for?" asked Haley.

"Well, I teach all my horses manners first. Then I look at what the horse likes to do. I try them out at everything. Some I train to compete. Rocky Mountains horses make terrific barrel racers and reiners. The taller ones can take on the big dressage horses. The horses who don't thrive in the show ring are better at working cattle or trail rides. Riding a gaited horse makes for a smoother ride if you're spending long hours in the saddle. A couple of horses I trained who belonged to other people went on to do eventing and endurance rides. They're just a great all around breed," said Sam, beaming.

There was a buzzing and Mom pulled a phone out of her purse. It took a while to sink in that her mom had a cell phone.

"Hello. Sure. Okay, wonderful. Can you put the box inside the coop for me. We'll be back soon. Keep the door shut so the heat stays in."

Mom paused. "No, don't open the box. They should be okay for a little longer. I'll be there soon."

Haley looked at her, head cocked.

"My chicks arrived."

"You sent away for chickens?" asked Haley.

"Yes, I've always wanted chickens. I got ten of them. They ship them. I'll need to get home and get them out of their box. Make sure they've got water and food. I've had heat lamps running in the coop for a few days now, part of the chicken tractor I built, getting it warmed up for them."

"Wow," said Haley. "We'd better get going then."

"I need to grab a few groceries at the store first," said Mom. "This is going to be so exciting to finally have chickens."

They went next door to the grocery store and rushed through it, picking up what Mom needed for the weekend guests. More salad greens, milk and another can of tomato sauce. They were in the truck heading home in less than ten minutes. At home, Mom rushed in the house, carrying a cloth bag of groceries.

Haley said, "Go. I'll put the groceries away and then come out. You go help her Trixie."

Trixie grinned and bounced out the back door, following her grandmother.

Haley put the perishable food in the fridge, leaving the rest on the kitchen counter. Then she went out to the red chicken coop, which was a little wooden house on wheels. The coop could be moved around a pasture so the chickens could eat bugs and fertilize the grass and still be safe from predators. When one patch of grass was exhausted, the coop was moved to another.

There was a human sized door on one side and windows to let in light. There was a ground level flap along one wall, that was closed. Surrounding the side with the flap, was a metal structure covered with heavy chickenwire. The whole thing could be lowered so it was flush to the ground or raised to roll around. Inside the coop, all the little chicks were stumbling around, pecking at the food, drinking water or falling asleep in little piles.

Mom had corralled them in a large aluminum livestock feeder about a foot and a half tall and two feet wide. On the bottom was some sort of shredded wood bedding. A heat lamp hung above it. The yellow fluffy chicks looked warm and cozy. There was enough room in the coop that Mom, Trixie and Haley could all stand up inside.

There were at least three different kinds of chicks. Mom reeled off the breed names, but they went in one ear and out the other for Haley. The chicks made tiny little cheeps.

"They are so cute," Mom said.

Trixie just smiled. She was sitting on her haunches watching the little creatures. Occasionally, she'd pick one up, stroke it and gently put it back down again. Mostly, she just watched.

"That's good. They need to be picked up when they're young. To become tame. They'll stay nice and cozy in here," said Mom. "When they're old enough and it's warm outside, I'll wheel them out into the horse pasture. The chickens will be protected from critters but still find lots of bugs to eat. And the horses will be entertained."

The next couple of days flew by. Haley collected information from Mom and took photos all around the ranch to use on the website. The satellite dish wouldn't be up till Monday. Haley wrote up some text on her computer and edited the photos, so things would be ready to load in to a website, once she had internet access.

She took Trixie riding, down towards the Blackfoot. Trixie was so excited. Jerry chose Fog, a strawberry roan, for Trixie.

"She's one of our older gals. Not spooky at all. She's nice and mellow. Your job is to make sure she doesn't spend all her time standing around eating."

Haley got Tansy, a lovely buckskin gelding, to ride. She hadn't been on a horse since the last time she was back home.

"I'm out of practice."

"She's a good 'un. She'll take care of you, so you can keep an eye on your daughter."

Jerry showed Trixie how to mount the horse, how to neck rein and all the other basics. Trixie swung up into the saddle, looking a little nervous. She was about normal height and weight for her age. Jerry adjusted the stirrups to fit her. Trixie seemed to quickly get used to Fog shifting her weight from side to side. Haley remembered when she'd first been on a horse. When it shifted its weight as it walked, she'd been delighted and exhilarated. But if you weren't expecting it, the movement was a bit jolting. Jerry led Fog around for a few minutes. Trixie was smiling.

"The first time out, just walk. No trotting, galloping, none of that. She might speed up a bit going downhill or uphill, but you just stick to the saddle like glue. Hang onto the horn if you have to. She'll stay with Tansy. They're good buddies."

Trixie nodded and smiled at Haley.

Haley headed out down the ranch's main dirt road towards the River Pasture. She wanted to see how high the Blackfoot was.

Tansy was indeed a lovely, mellow horse. All of Mom's horses had to be. She didn't need jumpy, nervous horses taking her guests out on trail rides.

The saddle leather creaked as the gelding walked. The horse's weight shifted back and forth, as one side of the body moved up and forward, then the other. Haley loosened up and let herself sway with the motion of the horse. It felt comfortable riding again. She had never been a great rider, like some of the other girls in school had been. She'd always had her nose in a book, while they were out practicing riding and barrel racing. Many of them had competed in the local rodeo. Haley hadn't dared. She was nowhere good enough.

The smell of pine hung in the air. The sun was out.

Chickadees flitted between the trees. A squirrel screamed at Trixie and Haley, telling them off. Trying to get them to leave

She'd forgotten how much she loved these pine woods. Ponderosa pines grew a couple hundred feet tall and their yellow-red bark looked like a million puzzle pieces put together. Beneath them grew: Oregon grape, prickly plants with sour berries and chokecherry, more sour berries and if one was lucky, wild strawberries with their small, sweet berries.

Her childhood and youth had been spent walking or running through these woods. Losing herself in thickets and in the long summers walking along the river, when it was at it's diminished size once the spring thaws ended. She collected interesting rocks and driftwood. Looked for frogs and toads. Found puddles filled with tiny fish, growing larger while they safely hidden until the river to rose again in spring and bigger fish might find them. Out in nature, Haley had always been entertained.

A patch of purple shooting stars were growing in a sunny meadow at the base of an aspen. Haley hadn't seen the delicate wildflowers since she'd left Montana. They were a lovely promise of lazy summer days to come.

She glanced back at her daughter. Trixie was mesmerized.

Haley realized again, that the closest Trixie had been to nature was walking through the arboretum or going to the zoo. In some ways she'd been an awful mother.

It took about twenty minutes to get down to the river. They stopped the horses on a cliff overlooking the water. The Blackfoot was raging through her wide channel. In the deep greenish brown waters, logs were tossed around, turning end on end. This spring, the river filled the entire stream bed, where in the summer, once the snow melt had rushed downstream, the water would shrink to about one-twentieth the size. Less than that during the really hot, dry summers.

The water roiled around piles of tree stumps and roots

caught during previous floods and piled along the banks. In a few months, the river would be clear showing off the jewel colored rocks, but today it was deep and filled with mud.

The power of the water both frightened and invigorated her.

On the far side a small herd of deer stood, drinking from the edge of the torrent. They stared at the humans for a long time.

Haley felt as if they were trying to tell her something. Something important about her life and how to change it. Make it better. Make up for all her mistakes. Before she could catch that thought, the deer vanished into the woods on the other side, as if they'd never been.

The whisper of a thought disappeared just as perfectly.

The river held a sort of vibrancy for her. It was so powerful, she couldn't help feeling alive when she was near it. Especially now, when it was at its most powerful and dangerous stage. It shocked her into life.

Haley had spent the last several years running away. Away from James and his abuse. Away from job after job, failure after failure. Always afraid James would find them, again. She'd even failed her daughter. If she'd left James earlier, Trixie would never have witnessed the abuse. If she'd had more money, they wouldn't have lived in such a divey area of Seattle, Trixie wouldn't have witnessed the murder which stole her speech.

If, if, if. ...

Haley had screwed up so badly she had to run home again in order to save the two of them. Except that it wasn't home. It felt strange being here as an adult. Not how she would have imagined her life at this age.

Well, now she'd have to turn everything around. Help Trixie find her voice again. Make a success of her own life. Become a self-sufficient adult again.

They rode along the river, following the dirt road. Haley

could see where the wild, grassy pastures had been eaten by the river. Huge chunks were just missing, the edges having slid into the river most every spring for years. Fenceposts stood, the cross bars tumbling down, a sad monument to humanity trying to prove it could outwit nature.

Farther upstream she could see where the river had diverted its course and left the land uncovered. It was all piles of downed trees, rocks and sand. Like Mom said, not good for grazing cattle on. Eventually, the wood would rot and break down, grasses and other plants would take over the sandy areas. Whether it was fertile enough for pasture grass was anyone's guess. But by then, the river might take it again.

They rode back to the horse paddock. An hour and a half was long enough for Trixie's first time in the saddle. The poor girl was walking bowlegged when she got down.

Jerry took the horses and showed Trixie how to unsaddle them and she helped him brush them before they were turned loose in the paddock.

On Friday, the two couples who were staying for a week showed up. They were older, perhaps in their fifties. The men were sportsmen and coming to scope out fishing holes for next month when fly fishing season opened. The two women were happy to sit and knit or walk around the ranch and coo at the baby chicks or the two foals.

Haley realized they were also just happy to have someone else do the cooking.

CHAPTER 6 ~ MABEL

MABEL WENT TO THE LINEN CLOSET AND GOT OUT HER money, hidden between the clean bath towels. The smell of freshly washed sheets filled her nose.

She opened the pink envelope, which had been part of an old stationary set. With most of them you always ran out of envelopes before paper. With this set she'd run out of the thick paper printed with pictures of flowers. So she decided to keep her money in the pink envelope.

She still had $3,376.00 left. That was good. She'd spent some on groceries. Gotten a few luxuries like a steak. Some tomatoes and an avocado to add to a green salad. A bottle of fancy ten dollar wine. How long had it been since she'd had wine?

She grilled the steak outside on the barbecue. Smoke filled the freezing air, but there was nothing like that flavor. Then she came back inside, shivering, threw another log on the crackling fire and pulled a tv tray up to the wood stove and ate dinner there. It wasn't long before the small two bedroom house warmed up. She'd be glad when summer finally got here.

She savored the flavor of the grilled beef cooked just right, not too raw, not too well done. And the lettuce, avocado, tomato and olive oil salad dressing. Plus the red wine. Her late husband had never liked red wine. Never liked alcohol at all. So she hadn't kept it around. She still rarely drank, but maybe she could keep a bottle of something around the house. Just for now and then. She didn't have to pinch her pennies quite so tightly anymore.

She should probably put some of that money into her savings account and earn interest. But then the government would just want to tax it and she was done paying those bastards in Washington any money she didn't have too. They'd just use it for another war. No, the money was better in her linen closet.

She sipped the wine and tasted the fruitiness of it. It was perfect with her steak. And the wine was made by some folks over on the Flathead, Jim at the grocery store told her. It was nice to support people here in Montana.

She was going to enjoy having a little money for once.

What else should she do with it?

CHAPTER 7 ~ HALEY

On Saturday, after lunch, Haley decided to go over to Sam's to talk about his website. Trixie was happily helping Dani wrangle horses and taking the two men on a trail ride. Mom was going along, too.

Haley squeezed into a pair of jeans, which had really grown too tight, slid on a blue t-shirt and her new boots. She ran her hands over the smooth leather. She loved them, but they sorely needed to be broken in.

Haley drove the two minutes to Sam's ranch, feeling guilty. Like she should have ridden a horse or walked or something.

She didn't find him at first, so she went around taking photos and getting a sense of the place. He'd built a huge indoor arena, completely made of wood and painted a forest green, as were the barns. The arena must come in handy in the winter. He'd still be able to keep working his horses. Outside would be too cold and the normal snow depth here was six feet.

Attached to the arena was a wide hallway that led into a large barn. Completely new construction, it looked pristine. Everything in its place. Large 12' by 12' stalls. A wash rack and a couple of closed doors which had brown and gold signs labeled

—*tack room* and *food storage*. The latter must be for grains and supplements. It wasn't big enough for hay. There was only one horse in a stall. It was a tall horse, at least 17 hands. Possibly a Danish Warmblood. Haley didn't know much about Rocky Mountain Horses, except for the chocolate coloring and flaxen mane and tail, and that they were shorter. The Warmblood must belong to someone else. Maybe he boarded horses while training them.

She finally found Sam out behind the barn, working what must have been a Rocky Mountain Horse in a round pen, fenced with metal bars instead of the standard three wooden rails for this part of the country for horses, like Mom's fencing. Sometimes for cattle, too. Sometimes people still used barbed wire for cattle. It was too dangerous for horses, they spooked too easily or tried to jump it and ended up getting all tangled and cut up by barbed wire. Cattle weren't as easily spooked and didn't try to jump high fences.

"Well hello," he said, walking over to the fence. His boots, jeans and blue shirt covered with dust.

The chocolate brown horse with flaxen mane and tail, that he'd been working with, followed Sam sniffing at his cowboy hat.

"Hi. Nice place you've got here."

"I kind of like it. What brings you over this way?"

"I thought I'd take a look around, take some photos. See how I could help you with your website."

"Great," he said, pushing his hat back off his sweating forehead.

"Monday afternoon, I'll have internet," she said.

He stared at her.

"What?" she asked.

"You've never gone a whole week without the internet, have you?"

"It's been a while. But I do need it to do my work."

"I can see that, but when was the last time you took a vacation?"

"I can't remember. It hasn't exactly been in my budget. Single mom and all that."

"Don't you get child support?" he asked.

"I don't want to have anything to do with her father. And neither does she."

"That bad, huh?"

"Worse than you can imagine. I don't want him, or any money he might have, in our lives."

"Okay."

She put her hands in her pockets and felt her face heating up.

"Sorry, too much information."

"People seem to do that around me," he said, rubbing the horse's head. He unclasped the halter and turned the horse loose in the round pen, then slid out between the rails.

She could smell the horse's sweat as he followed Sam around the fence. He stuck his head over the top of the fence and lipped Sam's shirt.

"Now stop that," said Sam, pushing the horse away.

The horse snorted and raced around the round pen kicking and bucking and acting spooked.

"He's only two. Still a baby in so many ways," said Sam.

Sam opened the round pen gate which led into a pasture. The horse he'd been working with ran out of the round pen. Sam closed the round pen gate and snapped the halter onto a post inside the round pen that couldn't be reached from the pasture. He walked down a gravel path next to the fence, motioning for her to follow.

The pasture had six other horses in it. The pasture was fenced with new wood posts and rails left unpainted. Rustic, but highly functional. Just like the rest of his ranch looked.

The horses were all the same rich chocolate color with

flaxen manes and tail. The young horse raced across the pasture and tried to stir things up with the other horses. One of them, very pregnant, kicked him in the chest and he settled down a bit and went away to roll in the grass.

"Guess she told him," said Haley.

"He's a good horse. He'll be awesome in a couple more years. He's just young. Needs to get some ya-ya's out."

Sam showed her around the ranch. His stallion was happily grazing amidst another small herd of mares in another pasture.

Haley took several pictures of him. He was magnificent.

"What's your main business?" she asked. "Training other people's horses and doing clinics or breeding and selling your own horses?"

"I want it to be about 50/50," he said. "Right now I do more training. The horse selling business hasn't really taken off yet, my stallion's still new and the young ones I've bought are just coming into their second year. I've got a herd to build. The economy's still not great around here. I do pick up a good horse now and then at auctions. Train them up and sell them, though. The clinics are only once a year or so."

She pulled out her phone and made a note of what he said.

"Wow, you really are technology woman, aren't you?"

"I love it. Doesn't mean I don't love nature too."

He smiled.

"You want a cup of coffee and to go take a look at the website?"

"Sure."

They walked up to the house and the concrete sidewalk to his house. He scraped his boots on the boot brush that sat next to the doormat, then wiped them on the mat.

"I'm too busy to be taking my boots off all the time and I hate tracking in stuff all over the floor," he said, in explanation.

Or was it a polite way to ask her to clean off her boots? She wiped them on the mat and followed him in.

Sam's house was a new craftsman style filled with windows which let in the light and the view. The inside felt warm and cozy. It was painted a green that echoed the pine needles outside and had hardwood floors, beams and moulding. The furniture was upholstered in a medium colored leather with tables formed of small branches, peeled and varnished. A stone wall and floor fashioned from river rocks filled a corner in which a new wood stove stood. A woven green rug held the room together.

It was beautiful and tasteful and reminded her of a magazine spread for the West's Best Houses. Not the ultra modern things. This house felt livable.

The living room opened into a dining room, kitchen and a large office area that held a desk which looked so tidy it seemed never used. A new computer with a large screen sat on the desk.

Sam clearly had money from somewhere. Was the training horses gig really that profitable?

The house smelled of wood and leather. Even the floor was clean. There was another smell, food. Beef cooking, and maybe tomatoes. Fresh flowers sat on the kitchen table.

Her mom didn't even have fresh flowers out in the middle of summer when they were there to cut. Did the little grocery store even carry them?

He flicked on the computer and checked his phone messages while waiting for it to start up. He wrote a couple of numbers down and went into the kitchen to get the coffee. A long bar with stools formed a semi barrier between the kitchen and office area. She leaned on the bar watching him pour coffee.

"Black or would you like some cream?"

"Real cream?"

"Real cream," he said. "Well, it's not fresh from a cow. It's from the store."

"I'll take cream."

A crockpot sat on the kitchen counter, the inside of the lid covered with condensing water. That's where the smell came from. He followed her gaze.

"I'm making pot roast. With tomatoes and olives. The farrier's coming late this afternoon and if I don't cook during the day, I won't get dinner. I'm sort of attached to the whole eating thing."

She nodded, took her coffee and walked over to the computer. He brought his coffee over and set it down on a coaster. Then standing there, he brought up the website.

It was awful. The photos were blurry, the font terrible and whoever designed it must have been color blind.

She sat at the desk and wandered around the website, looking at the various pages. The information seemed skimpy, not what she'd need to know before buying a horse from a stranger.

"You need an overhaul. When was this one done?"

"Two, maybe three years ago."

"It doesn't reflect what I see on your property."

"What do you see?" he asked.

"I see an attention to detail, incredibly well done maintenance and stunning horses. Your barn is so clean you could eat off the floor. Nothing out of place. All the buildings are beautiful and everything I've seen on your property speaks of quality and care. This website looks outdated, sloppy and doesn't have enough information."

"You're hired," he said. "A friend of a friend did it. I was busy moving and getting fencing and buildings up.

"Did you build all this?"

"I helped with the building a bit. I was the contractor and designer. I hope never to be doing all those things at once, ever again."

She laughed. "I don't know how you survived."

She made a few other suggestions and asked a lot of questions. He liked her suggestions and she told him what she charged. He agreed and said he'd make up a list of information about the horses he wanted to put up for sale.

The front door flew open and in swaggered a tall, thin woman with shoulder-length blonde hair and bright blue eyes. She was dressed completely in white. Blindingly so. Her perfume preceded her into the room. She dropped her purse on the coffee table and strode over to hug Sam.

Clearly, they knew each other well. And just when Haley was beginning to like him. To see possibilities.

"Hi Sam," she said.

"Julianna, this is Haley from next door. Haley, this is Julianna. Haley's going to redo my website."

"Nice to meet you," said Haley, shaking her hand.

"I'm so glad you're going to fix that awful website. I've been telling him he needed to do that for over a year now."

"Well, I'd better get back. Mom's got things for me to do. I'll start work on this later in the week. And once I've got email working again on my computer, you can email me any photos with descriptions for the individual horses you want to put up on it."

"Sounds like a plan," he said.

She set her empty cup on the bar and left.

All the way home she felt annoyed. It wasn't a good idea to get involved with one's clients. Not beyond being friendly. Why had she even considered such a thing?

Because it had been so many years since she'd had any romantic relationship and look how that one turned out. The only thing good to come of it was Trixie.

By the time she got home, Mom was ensconced in the kitchen. Haley loved this house, but everything looked shabby in comparison to Sam's. The house was older and even though it had been well maintained, it hadn't held up. It needed updating. That involved money which Mom probably didn't have.

Where Sam's house looked spacious and serene, Mom's

house looked cramped and overly busy. Her belongings needed editing. Outside would benefit from a landscape designer coming through and cleaning things up. And the outbuildings, …

She sighed and put her purse in her room. Then put on an apron and helped Mom in the kitchen.

"Where's Trixie?"

"Out in the chicken coop. She's taking good care of those chicks, making sure they're not afraid of people."

Haley laughed.

"She has a real gift with animals, you know," said Mom.

"I didn't. She's never really been around animals."

Dinner was grilled steak, baked potatoes and a green salad. She'd talked Mom into buying some wild greens at the grocery store. Mom had been dubious.

Haley washed the greens and spun them dry. Then she chopped up some green onions and tossed in some dried cranberries she'd also made Mom buy. She added some slivered almonds and made a balsamic vinegar/olive oil dressing. Haley tossed the salad and sprinkled on some freshly grated parmesan.

She cleaned off the dining room table and fluffed a white linen tablecloth over it. Then put out white cloth napkins and set the table. The interesting thing was that having a bed and breakfast forced Mom to get out the good china, the real silver and crystal. Haley had seen them used maybe twice during her childhood.

When she'd asked Mom about that, her response was "I'm not getting any younger. I decided that the china and silver needed to be used. And you know, there's been no breakage. Not like I expected. Of course I don't put them in the dishwasher. But they really do make the dinners seem almost elegant. The guests really like seeing the old china."

Haley opened a couple of bottles of wine, red and white. The wine was from California. She decided she should search out some of the Montana wines. See if they could buy them by the case. Maybe putting a focus on using more locally sourced food could be one of the selling points for the business.

She pulled her phone out her pocket and added that to the list of things to do.

"How was Sam?" asked Mom.

"I didn't know he was so well off."

"I think he's mostly made good money and always invested it. He advised me on some investments after Glen died. Plus he did a lot of the work himself."

"But he hired an interior designer didn't he?"

"His sister. She's got her own business in Denver. I think she helped with designing the barn and other outbuildings too."

"Have you seen that arena?"

"Lovely, isn't it?" said Mom.

"The whole place is amazing."

"It is very pretty," said Mom.

"But what?"

"Well, I couldn't live there. It'd be like living in a magazine. Everything's new. I'd be afraid I'd scratch the floor or mar the leather couch."

"Is he that anal?"

"What do you mean?" Mom scrunched up her face in confusion.

"Is Sam that much of a clean freak?"

"I don't think so. He has a housecleaner. Trudy goes in once a week and cleans for him. I just meant because it's all new. Trouble and Twinkletoes would shed everywhere. Twinkletoes would make short work of all that new leather, I think. Trouble would scratch up a new floor. I like my lived-in house."

"Okay, so we can cross off house remodel from the to-do list."

"Well, there are a few things I'd like to change, but the money's not there yet. Things could stand to be repainted, things like that. It would be good for business and I could probably take it off on my taxes."

"You just took a class, didn't you?"

"Yes, Winnie and I drove to Helena and took a couple of business classes. I learned a lot about taxes."

"We should sit down some time, maybe week after next, when the guests are out and go over your list of things you want to do. See if we can make a timeline for them."

"That sounds fun. Well, I'd better get out back and grill those steaks. Can you put the sour cream in a bowl and out on the table? Keep an eye out for that cat. She likes to explore the table. I think there may be some chives ready to cut in the vegetable garden. Those can go in a separate little bowl. Some of the guests might not care for them."

"Will do."

Haley went into the dining room and found Twinkletoes trying to drag a napkin off the table.

"No! Go find some of your toys and play with those. The table is off limits," she said, picking up the fuzzy cat and putting her in the living room.

She straightened the table, then went out to cut some chives.

She could hardly wait till she was online again. She wanted to get to work on the websites.

CHAPTER 8 ~ MABEL

Mabel sat in the green Jeep Wagoneer this time, outside another old drugstore in another small town. She tapped her fingers on the steering wheel. Then put her thin leather gloves on and got out.

It wasn't icy on the street, just muddy and slushy from all the snow melt. Rubber boots kept her feet dry. The air smelled clean from the chinook which had blown through, melting everything.

Mabel wore her thin blue scarf over the brown wig again, the scarf tied beneath her chin. And a short, navy wool coat over navy slacks. She looked like any other old woman trying to keep up appearances.

She walked inside the drugstore. It was laid out much the same as the last one. Lots of short shelves crammed into the center of the store. She went straight to the beauty products and lingered. Looking around. Her mouth felt dry and pasty.

'I'm invisible,' she said to herself.

A young mother with a fussy baby stood at the checkout counter. Talking to the young woman with spiky black hair who worked there. The only two people in the store. There weren't any security cameras.

The drugstore was old and rundown. Tan paint peeled off the walls. The linoleum was cracked. It even smelled old. Mildewy. Would it have enough money?

The young mother left the store. Mabel moved quickly to the counter.

She pulled out her gun. Held it in front of her. Not visible from the side, should someone enter the store.

"Put all your money in a bag and hand it to me."

The young woman who worked there stared at her, mouth open.

"Do it. Don't press an alarm. Just give me the money!"

The woman, startled out of paralysis, rushed to open the cash register. Shoved the money into a white plastic bag.

"Get the big bills under the tray too," said Mabel.

The woman lifted the tray and pulled out a stack of 50's and 100's. Shoved those into the bag. She handed the bag to Mabel.

"Give me your phone and get down on the floor."

"I don't have my phone. It's in my locker."

"Get down on the floor and stay there for ten minutes. Don't call anyone or ring an alarm."

The woman got down on the floor. Mabel fled the store. Heart pounding.

Inside the Jeep, she turned it on, then shifted into gear. Forgetting to fasten her seatbelt until miles down the road. In Missoula.

She slid off the wig and scarf. Pulled over to top off the tank at a gas station. Slipped off her coat inside the car and got out wearing her red sweater and pants. It was chilly, but she needed to look different. While the gas was pumping, she took the money out of the plastic bag and tossed the bag in a garbage can. Put the money in her purse. Then took off her leather gloves, tucking them in the purse.

Paid for gas with cash from her wallet and was on the road in less than two minutes.

Two hours later, she was home.

$7,296.82 richer.

She smiled, looking at the money.

That would make a nice contribution to the new roof fund for the elementary school. The one the town had tried desperately to fund for years. The one the state and federal governments couldn't or wouldn't help with.

CHAPTER 9 ~ HALEY

THE MONDAY MORNING AFTER THE WEEKEND GUESTS WERE gone, preparations for the next round of people, who would be arriving Wednesday, had begun. Haley and Trixie stripped the beds and began washing load after load of bedding. The smell of laundry soap permeated the house. It was awful and overpowering. Haley made a note on the grocery list to buy soap that was unscented.

Then they thoroughly cleaned the two rooms. Even using antibacterial wipes on doorknobs and dresser drawer pulls. The other rooms in the house were dusted and vacuumed as well. The common areas spiffed up.

Haley was finally able to get away after lunch. Trixie headed out to watch Sam work with the foals. Haley needed to do her own work.

She sat at her computer, writing website copy in a word doc, for Mom's potential website. It wasn't going so well.

"Lincoln, Montana. Home of the Unibomber and only eighteen miles west of Roger's Pass, which holds the record for the coldest temperature ever recorded in the lower forty-eight states, -70 degrees Fahrenheit on January 20, 1954."

Crap, that'll never sell the place. She needed to be writing on the actual website. That's when her magic happened. She glanced at the computer clock. 3 p.m. The satellite installer should arrive any time.

Haley stopped typing and went to the kitchen for a fresh cup of coffee. She felt drawn to the window, but couldn't see the pasture from there. Taking her cup of coffee outside, she walked across the road to the pasture. At the far end, Sam squatted down and was rubbing his hands over a foal's entire body. Trixie was doing the same with the other foal. The mares stood nearby, watching intently. The other horses were either grazing or sleeping.

Mom was cleaning up and repairing tack out in the barn, getting everything ready for the busy season. She was beginning to get reservations for every weekend and halfway through May, full week reservations were beginning to come in for the summer.

What she needed was a draw in the winter. Lincoln's airport was large enough to fly people in. If Haley could find a charter company that they could team up with, make a package with that might work. Fly people in from Missoula, Great Falls, Helena, Billings. A winter getaway to do what? Sit by the fire? Drink hot chocolate, perhaps laced with alcohol? Sit in a hot tub and look at the snow?

Maybe sleigh rides? Get a couple of wooly draft horses to pull it. They had always used a snow plow on all the roads around the property. They needed to get feed to the cattle and horses. So, a sleigh might not work.

Snowshoeing. They could offer that. Beautiful scenery. The Blackfoot was beautiful in any weather. She'd have to talk to Mom about it.

A tall, gangly man appeared from around the front of the house. He wore a uniform with the name of the satellite company on it. Haley almost bounced up and down with relief.

A couple of hours later, Haley was hooked up and online. Her fingers flew across the keyboard. She felt a surge of energy move through her as she focused on the tasks at hand.

She'd registered her business with the state and bought domain names for Mom and Winnie. Mom's website was beginning to take shape.

"Haley, dinner," called Mom from the kitchen.

Haley groaned. She didn't want to stop. It seemed like months since she'd been able to work. And this was just the type of work she loved.

But her stomach rumbled. The smell of roast chicken had been seeping down the hallway for quite some time.

Sadly, she logged out of the site and put her computer to sleep, patting it as she got up. She closed the door to her room, not trusting Twinkletoes or Trouble. Trixie always left her door open and nearly all her socks had gone missing.

Haley sat down at the dining room table. Mom was just putting some mashed potatoes on the table. Trixie was pouring a glass of milk for herself. Mom stood there and cut slices of the chicken, then cut off the thighs, setting one of Trixie's plate.

"Well, both you girls are beaming today. You must have had good days," said Mom.

Trixie nodded her head enthusiastically.

"You had fun playing with the foals today?" asked Haley, piling slices of the chicken on her own plate.

Trixie nodded and dished up potatoes and gravy.

"I sure had fun getting started on your website," said Haley to Mom.

"You'll have to show me how to work the internet. I haven't a clue. I suppose I should buy a computer, shouldn't I?"

"I guess you should. I'll see what I can find online."

"The world has changed so much. I don't know if I'll ever get used to buying things I've never even seen."

"Mom, they've had mail order catalogs since the 1800's."

"Well, that's true. Mabel has a book reader machine. She buys books and they magically appear on her machine. And then she can read it without ever leaving home. It's that instant gratification thing. I'm not sure it's healthy for the human race."

"Well, it is wonderful to be able to have all this technology. Photos can be taken and sent around the world at the snap of your fingers. So can news. You can watch a volcano erupting halfway around the planet, just like that."

"Well, the world changes. Nothing we can do about that, just have to roll with it."

The door opened and Jerry and Dani came in the back.

"Sorry we're late," said Jerry. "Had a little emergency fence repair."

"Where?" asked Mom.

"Out in the big pine pasture," said Jerry. "A tree fell on the fence and broke the top two rails. No cattle escaped though. It's all fixed now."

"Good," said Mom.

They sat down and food was passed around again. The roast chicken was moist and luscious. And Mom's gravy was to die for. Haley was sure her jeans would soon become too tight between Mom's great cooking and Winnie's desserts.

"Sam was asking where you were," said Mom to Haley.

"I've been inside working all day," she said. "And then the satellite guy came, so I helped him figure out where to wire things. We'll need to check and see if my router reaches the cabins. If not, we might need to get a stronger one."

She didn't want to think about Sam. Haley wasn't going to get involved with anyone and she needed to cool things off a bit.

"Sam says he'll send you the information you asked for."

"Okay. He told me that yesterday."

"I think he wanted to see you," said Mom.

"He saw me yesterday."

"He's sweet on you."

"Mom."

"We're all family here."

Jerry and Dani nodded.

"He already has a girlfriend."

"No. Who?" asked Mom.

"I saw her yesterday. Juliana. Didn't catch her last name. Drives a white Jag. Fancy dresser."

My god, she was beginning to talk like she used to when she was a kid. Regressing.

Mom laughed.

"Juliana is his older sister. She lives in Denver and comes up now and then. She helped design his house and the other buildings. She's an interior designer."

Haley tried not to let her mouth flop open. His sister. Hm. She didn't look like his sister. Too glamorous. So where did that leave her feelings?

She still shouldn't get involved with him. He was a client now.

The rest of the week passed quickly. The house was filled with the smells of Mom baking apple pies and marinating meats.

And laundry soap. The ever present soapy smell. Haley couldn't wait till the stinky stuff was gone. Mom had agreed to buy unscented next, but she'd already stocked up on the old soap. Being a child of the depression meant never wasting a thing.

Haley was lost in a haze of helping clean around the house, cooking and getting ready for the next guests. She spent as much time as she could working on Mom's website. By Friday, she had it up and running. The reservation system wasn't working though.

No matter what she tried it messed up. She tried different

programs, none of them seemed to work. She decided to give it a rest for a few days. At least the basic website was up and running. Mom was thrilled by it.

She ordered a computer for Mom. It was just easier since the nearest computer store was over a hundred miles away. It would be another week or so till it arrived. Mom wasn't ready to deal with reservations anyway. Since they were so close to the busy season beginning, she was thinking Mom wouldn't have time to really learn how to use it till next fall or winter.

Mom spent nearly all her time working. She was always cleaning something. Or fixing something else. Or organizing cupboards or the feed room in the barn. Or taking care of the chicks, who were growing at an amazing rate. They were beginning to get actual feathers now, some white, some brown, some black.

Mom worked way too hard. The only time she rested was to sleep. And that wasn't for eight hours either.

"You know older people don't need as much sleep," Mom said.

"That's a myth. Older people just don't sleep as well, so they think they need less sleep."

"I'm doing fine," said Mom. "It feels good to stay busy. And I do go out for coffee sometimes."

That much was true. Haley and Trixie had only been there a week and a half and Mom had gone for coffee three times with Mabel.

The woman was an enigma to Haley. Her former high school English teacher, who'd seemed so prim and proper was actually quite the wild woman. Her husband had died about ten years ago after fighting cancer for decades. Mabel was in her seventies and apparently, always on the go. She was always driving off to another town to visit someone or go shop in Missoula or even Great Falls.

Even in winter when the roads were dicey. The woman had snow tires and wasn't about to sit around at home.

Mabel was waiting for some money to come in, Mom had said. She didn't know if it was inheritance or some sort of financial settlement, but apparently there was money in her future, which was good. She had been struggling for a long time to make ends meet. How she could do so much on social security was a mystery.

"Of course, her house is probably paid off," said Mom. "But her husband didn't leave much money behind when he died. Just lots of medical bills. And she has a few health problems, expensive prescriptions."

Mabel stopped over to bring Mom some cinnamon rolls from Winnie.

The angular old woman stood in the kitchen. She was a little shorter than Haley, but she must have shrunken with age. She'd always seemed so tall.

"Mabel, sit down, have a cup of coffee," said Mom.

"Oh, I don't want to keep you. I know you've got guests coming today."

"Well, they're not here yet. Thanks for bringing the cinnamon rolls. Saves me a trip into town. Our guests will love them tomorrow morning."

"Nobody makes them like Winnie."

Haley's mouth was watering just looking at the box.

"Don't you dare," said Mom. "Those are for tomorrow."

Haley poured a cup of coffee instead and looked out the window.

Trixie was out with the horses.. Sam was here again today. He was showing her how to lead the foals around.

She watched them for a few minutes, catching the middle of Mom and Mabel's conversation.

"You know, the older you get, the more invisible you are."

"No," said Mom.

"It's true. It started when I was about forty-five. Men didn't look at me any more. Neither did women for that matter. There were never any compliments on my clothes or jewelry. If I hadn't still been a teacher standing at the front of a classroom, no one would have looked at me at all. As I got older, I noticed it even more. My friend in Havre, Essie, says the same. The things that she gets away with. And it's true. I went to a community meeting last month and I dressed up like I was going to the fanciest place ever. Makeup, a dress, even stockings and dressy shoes. Wore my best jewelry. No one noticed. No one said a thing. So, the next meeting, I wore torn jeans, my work boots, a shabby t-shirt and and old raggedy sweater on top. Even put a bandana over my hair. Same thing. Not a word."

"That's interesting," said Mom.

"I tell you, old women are invisible. Invisibility is my superpower. I bet I could rob a bank and get away with it."

"I wouldn't try it," said Mom. "They've got cameras, I think. The cameras would see you."

"Well, I'm not about to. Robbing a bank is stupid. Too much security. You're right. It's not like in the '30's. When you could get away with things like that if you were smart."

"So, what's up at Winnie's?" asked Mom, very obviously changing the subject.

They began to talk about people Haley didn't know. George and Ethel had just come back from Arizona, where they wintered, to find a bear had broken into their house and trashed it.

"That's awful," said Mom.

"I know. Well, they've been busy cleaning up. Put a metal door in this time. I don't know what the bear was smelling, because they were gone. Only had some instant food left in their cupboards, Ethel said. Such a shame. Their house always looked so nice."

Haley took the opportunity to go back and work on Mom's

website, but she still couldn't make the reservation piece function right. She downloaded another piece of software. Perhaps that would do the trick. She'd try it tomorrow.

She began to work on Winnie's website. Putting in photos and the menu. It came together fairly quickly. She thought about adding a place for the daily specials, but decided against it. If people had to actually go to the cafe to find out the specials and weren't interested in them, there would be no way they'd leave. Not after smelling the food. They'd stay and have something else. Too bad she couldn't bottle that.

She put in a section for testimonials instead. Those would be easy to collect.

Trixie came rushing into Haley's room, her face luminous.

"What's up, honey?"

Trixie typed a message onto the note app on her phone and held it up for Haley to read.

"I led a foal around!!!!!!!"

"That's awesome. Was it fun?"

Trixie nodded enthusiastically, then ran back out of the room.

Haley sighed deeply.

When would her daughter speak again?

CHAPTER 10 ~ MABEL

MABEL STOPPED AT WINNIE'S FOR A CUP OF COFFEE AND A piece of pie. The smells of bacon and strong coffee filled the warm air.

It was Thursday afternoon almost a week after her last heist. She sat at a table by herself. Everyone in the packed cafe was a stranger. Tourists. She knew Bea's daughter Haley had made a website for the cafe. Maybe it was working.

She hoped so. She wanted the cafe to thrive but one of these days she might have to make a reservation. Now that would be something.

Winnie was waiting tables and came over with a glass of water.

"Good afternoon Mabel, pie and coffee?"

"Yes please. What have you got today?"

"Huckleberry, lemon meringue, pear anise and chocolate silk cream pie."

"Ooh, I think I'll have the chocolate silk. That sounds delicious."

"I think you'll like it," said Winnie. "As soon as I get caught up I'll come set a spell."

"Oh good. Busy day today."

"It's been wild. Everybody and their brother has come in."

Mabel nodded, sipped the water which tasted strongly of minerals, just like her own, and opened her purse. She took a map from her purse and spread it out on the table.

Where should she go tomorrow?

There'd been a small article in the paper about the last one. No real details, except that the robber had been an elderly woman. Same with the news on a Missoula station. They hadn't interviewed the young woman who worked at the drug store.

She'd pull one more robbery and then wait for a long time. Unless something came up that needed a lot of money.

Winnie came by with the pie and a mug of coffee.

"You planning another trip?"

"I think I'll head down to Bozeman to visit my niece and her kids tomorrow. I'm getting cabin fever."

Mabel took a bite of the pie. It was rich and chocolatey. Intense and balanced with the real whipped cream on top. She smiled and said, "This is divine Winnie."

"Thank you. That's a long drive. You better take along a thermos of coffee."

"Oh, I will. Might even stay over. In a hotel. That would be fun."

"I'd sure like to go on a vacation. Too much work around here. No rest for the wicked," Winnie smiled and moved along to pour coffee at other tables.

Mabel looked at the map.

She wasn't going to Bozeman. She'd go somewhere around Great Falls. Find a small town on the way with a likely looking drugstore.

Maybe put a large donation in the tip jar someday when Winnie wasn't looking.

CHAPTER 11 ~ HALEY

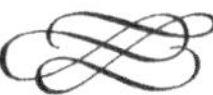

IT WAS SATURDAY AFTERNOON. MOM'S PLACE WAS JAMMED with people who were all inside because of the rain.

It didn't rain that much in Montana, not compared to Seattle. Trixie was holed up in her room, absorbed in a book.

Mom had set up card tables in what had once been Haley's playroom. Since Mom started the B and B, the room had been used for the occasional dance, but mostly for entertainment. The room was large with wood floors and mostly empty. She'd put three wood shelves against three of the walls which held games, puzzles and books and were topped with vases of blue silk flowers. Haley wanted to change the fake flowers to real ones, but hadn't figured out a way to gracefully tell Mom she needed to update her decorating to something a bit classier. Today, the guests were playing cards or working on puzzles, she could hear the laughter all the way in her room. Happy guests even in the rain, that was good.

Mom was cooking dinner, the smells of her red sauce permeated the house. Pungent oregano and rich basil made her mouth water.

Haley had cabin fever. She felt anxious and antsy, tapping

her short fingernails on the table holding her laptop. She wanted to go for a walk, but not in the rain.

She decided to go into town and talk with Winnie about her website. She wanted to take a photo of Winnie, and her husband and chief cook, Eddy, for the website.

Half an hour later, she pulled up in front of Winnie's. At three in the afternoon, there was still a sizable crowd.

Haley walked inside, waved at Winnie who was busy taking orders and took a seat. She perused the specials menu and decided on Huckleberry pie with ice cream. The other server, Gina, took her order.

Haley was deep in huckleberry and vanilla ice cream goodness, when Winnie finally came and sat down.

"Whoo. I'm pooped. It's been a crazy busy day."

"That's a good thing, right?"

"If I've got the staff for it. Mary's out sick, but we've passed the worst of it. I'm glad Gina could stay late though. It'll be a while before Eddy is free enough to take photos."

"It's okay. I'm just eating pie. I can wait."

"I don't mean to pry, but are you expecting someone to come out to see you from Seattle?"

"What do you mean?" asked Haley, her eyes narrowing.

"Well, a man came in one day last week, asking for you. Said he'd heard you were back here and he was just driving through. Wanted to see you. I said I hadn't heard you'd been back. He said he'd wanted to surprise you and asked me to give him a call if I saw you. I've put his card somewhere for you. He seemed a bit dodgy to me, so I didn't tell him the truth."

"What was his name?" asked Haley. Her entire body tensed up.

"I can't remember. It was a real common first name, but formal. I can go look for the card."

"James? James Jackson?"

Winnie said, "That's it. That was his name. Are you okay?"

Haley's muscles tightened as a wave of fear passed through her. She forced herself to take a deep breath.

Haley put her hand on Winnie's arm and said. "Please do not tell him you've seen me. Or Trixie. We're definitely not in town. He is such bad news."

Winnie said, "Honey, I'm glad I trusted my instincts. He seemed like he was going to keep coming back. What do you want me to do? Should I sick Eddy on him?"

"I think you should just pretend you haven't see me in twenty years and have no idea where I might have gone. Or perhaps you heard I went to Florida, got a job there."

"That bad, huh?"

"He's my abusive ex, and Trixie's dad. We left when she was young, but she remembers him. I never want to see him again. I even took a restraining order out on him, once upon a time. It's probably expired now."

Winnie gave a quiet long whistle.

"When was this?" asked Haley.

"He came in on Wednesday, I think."

She'd put up her own website for her business on Monday afternoon. Soaring Eagle Website Design. She hadn't used her own name, but she did have her own distinctive stamp. He'd worked with computers too and might have figured it out. Could have remembered she was from here and may have been looking for tech people working in the area, hoping to find her.

But why was he looking for her after all these years? Or was he looking for Trixie? Did he have a sudden desire to be a father?

Haley's rage mingled with the fear.

It was unlikely he wanted to be Trixie's dad. People changed, but not that much. And it didn't really matter why. Haley had done everything she could to keep Trixie safe. Put her in a place where she could finally feel safe again and maybe even begin to speak.

"I'm sorry. I didn't mean to upset you," said Winnie. "I think you should tell everyone you know about him. Make sure they keep an eye out for strangers hanging around."

"It's just so embarrassing," said Haley.

"I know honey, but everyone makes mistakes. That's how we learn, by screwing up. This one shouldn't be allowed to haunt you forever."

Haley nodded, her stomach knotted up. The pie and ice cream roiled around in her belly, threatening to come back up.

"Honey, you don't look well. You're white as a sheet. Why don't I get someone to drive you home? I can bring your car out tomorrow. There's Sam. Sam, can I ask you for a favor?"

Haley tried to get a word in, but Winnie didn't stop talking.

"Sam, could you drive Haley home? She's not doing so well. Honey, give me your keys and I'll make sure you get your car back."

Sam said, "I'd be happy to drive you home."

Haley shook her head.

"Now don't argue with me. Hand over the keys," said Winnie.

Haley gave her the keys and then said, "Washington plates."

"I'll move your car around back. No one goes back there. We'll bring it out to Bea's as soon as we leave here."

"I'm okay, really. I can drive."

"No, you're not okay," said Sam "Winnie's right. You're pure white and you're shaking. Let me do you a favor."

She followed him out to the front room. Gina handed him a bag of food and he waved goodbye.

Haley looked around outside, but she had no idea what type of car James drove these days. She should ask Winnie. She hurried into Sam's green pickup and they drove off.

"What's got you so rattled?" he asked.

She didn't want to tell him. She felt stupid. But she was afraid Winnie was right. People needed to know. To be able to look out for them. It wasn't just her. She needed to keep Trixie safe.

So, she told him. Everything. Once she opened her mouth it all spilled out between sobs.

"We were married. It was nice at first. We both worked with computers, had unreasonable hours but were making tons of money. I got pregnant and there was Trixie. But then the big .coms starting crashing. James got laid off. I was still working. He couldn't get a job. He started drinking heavily and became verbally abusive. I don't think he ever hurt Trixie, but he sure wasn't reliable childcare either. I loved him, stupidly thought he could change. That he just needed to get back on his feet again."

She continued, "One day when I got home from working late, he accused me of having an affair. As if I had time for that sort of thing. Anyway, he hit me. Several times. Trixie saw it, I think she was three. He bloodied up my face, broke a few bones and dislocated my shoulder. A neighbor heard us and called the cops. I ended up in the hospital, James landed in jail. A friend took Trixie for a couple of days. I pressed charges and filed for divorce the same day. When I got out of the hospital, Trixie and I moved out. I changed jobs so he wouldn't find us. I ended up doing that a lot. I never found a job where I could completely work from home. He was always able to hunt us down."

She sobbed and wiped off her face, then began again. "The next few years were awful. The tech industry was crashing, big time. I became known for quitting jobs. As soon as he tracked me down, I'd quit and Trixie and I would run away again. The tech community was small enough, word got around that I wasn't reliable. No one would hire me. We moved house a lot. I began waitressing, because he wouldn't look for me there. We lived in cheaper and cheaper housing as we burned through my savings. I'd divorced him, but there was no money coming from him. His job situation was worse than mine, I think. Anyway, we were living in an apartment complex that was a dive. There were lots of drugs. That was about two years ago. Trixie hated school, she was being bullied, afraid to stand up for herself. She came home from school one day, went to the neighbor's, the one who took care of her after school. I was at work. She saw the neighbor murdered. I don't know exactly what happened. By the time I got home, Trixie was huddled in her closet crying. She hasn't spoken since. She'd never talked a lot, not since the day he beat me up. Her whole world was ripped apart the day he did that. So after the neighbor was murdered we picked up and moved again. I pulled her out of school and began homeschooling her. I took her to psychologists. We kept moving to cheaper places where I could afford the rent. I kept waiting tables, leaving her with friends while I worked. She was afraid to be alone. She's gotten better about that part, at least. After Dad died, I decided to come back here. I just couldn't make ends meet anymore in Seattle. Not on a waitress' wages. And I was afraid he'd find us again."

She took a deep breath and let it out slowly. She hadn't told anyone. Ever. Trixie had been the only one who had therapy, that's where all the money had gone. Never for her.

Sam pulled into Mom's driveway and parked.

"That's awful. You've been carrying it around for a long time, haven't you?"

She nodded, her face wet from tears. He brushed her tears away with the back of his hand.

"Well, we've got to keep him away from the two of you, that's for sure. I think you should talk to the Sheriff. Get a restraining order. See if you can find a current photo of him online somewhere and pass it around. It would be helpful if everyone knew what he looked like. Chances are he's just passing through."

"No. It's not just chance. He's a city boy. There's nowhere for him to pass through to."

"Fair enough. We've got to get him out of town. We'll see what we can do. Does Bea keep any alcohol around?"

"Yeah, why?"

"I think you need a stiff drink," he said, getting out of the truck.

She got out and said, "Now's not the time to tell her. She's busy with guests. I don't want Trixie to know. She's just beginning to settle in, to feel safe again."

"This is a secret you can't keep from her. If this man's looking for her, she needs to know."

Haley felt so confused. Would it do any good to tell Trixie? She wasn't sure. She knew it would scare her. This was just so unfair to her daughter. Why had she been so stupid?

Inside the house, Mom was in the kitchen.

"Oh Haley, the computer and printer arrived. I didn't unwrap them. They're in your room." Mom stared at her. "What's wrong?"

Haley didn't know what to say.

Sam said, "I think we all need to talk. Trixie included. Some place private."

"We can go into the office," said Mom. "Trixie's outside with the chicks."

"I'll go get her and meet you in the office," said Sam. "Bring a bottle and some glasses."

Mom gave him a strange look as he went out the back door. Haley trudged into the office like a child at school and on her way to the Principal's office. She sat in one of the cushioned desk chairs by the wood shelves filled with business ledgers.

Mom followed bringing a bottle of whiskey and three glasses. She poured one and handed it to Haley. Haley sniffed and held the glass between her two hands. Sam and Trixie came in and shut the door.

Sam pointed at Haley, and said, "Drink it."

Haley sighed and sipped some of the whiskey, feeling it

tickle her nose, then gasped as it slid down her throat, burning. Trixie sat next to Haley and took her hand, looking worried. Haley began to cry.

She couldn't even speak. Sam told Mom and Trixie what Haley had told him. Mom was sitting at the desk, her head in her hands. Occasionally, during the long tale, Haley sipped her whiskey. When Sam had finished, he drank his in one swallow.

Trixie began shaking. Haley put her arm around her, then pulled Trixie onto her lap and rocked her.

"I really didn't think he'd find us here," Haley said.

The room was filled with silence for a few minutes, then Mom said, "Well hell. We need a plan to take care of this jackass once and for all."

CHAPTER 12 ~ MABEL

MABEL STOPPED AT WINNIE'S ON HER WAY BACK HOME. SHE felt too tired from driving to make dinner. She'd have a burger as a late lunch, early dinner. It was 3:30, just under the wire.

She parked the dark blue Suburban out in front. It was filthy, from the melting snow and dirty sand used to create traction on icy roads. Now that she was finished for a while, all the cars could be washed off. Mac would have been horrified at them sitting around covered with mud. It ruined their paint, he'd said.

Then again, he would have been even more horrified at her activities. The only thing she regretted was scaring the poor employees. The young kid today had been terrified. He'd stammered and stuttered.

She'd been kind. Helping him along. She'd gotten a lot of money from that drugstore. As well as a pack of spearmint gum, that she was still chewing.

Mabel got out of the car and left her purse inside, just taking a ten dollar bill and the car keys with her. She locked the car and walked around puddles to the cafe.

It was almost empty. Winnie and Eddy were the only ones working.

"Well, hi stranger," said Winnie. "You back in town."

"Yes, it was a long drive back. I thought I'd grab an early dinner here before you close. I'm too pooped to cook."

"Do you know what you want?" asked Eddie, peering out from the kitchen.

"I'll just take a cheeseburger," she said, sitting down at a table, and peeling her coat off. The cafe was warm from the ovens running all day. "And a chocolate shake. If you need to close, I'll take it to go."

"No, you're fine eating here." Winnie sat down with her. "How was your trip?"

"It was lovely. I haven't seen my niece or her children for years. The kids are almost out of elementary school." Mabel didn't like lying, but it had to be done and she was good at it. She knew how to do it right, after watching so many school kids fail at lying for all those years.

"Oh, I'm glad you had fun."

The front door swung open.

Winnie got up and said, "I'll go get your shake."

A short, thin man walked in. He had stubble, most of the young men did these days. A style Mabel hated. It made them look indecisive, as if they couldn't decide whether to be clean shaven or grow a beard. He was well dressed in new jeans, a tailored, light blue shirt covered with a blue fleece jacket.

He asked Winnie, "Have you'd heard anything about Haley and her daughter."

Who was this man? Mabel didn't like him. He had an imperious tone to his voice.

She watched Winnie stiffen and say, "Not a thing."

That was interesting. Winnie didn't like him either. Not enough to tell him the truth.

"So, they haven't moved back here?"

"No," said Winnie.

If Winnie didn't want him to know then he must be bad news. Winnie wasn't a good liar though. Never had been.

Mabel said, "I talked to her Mom the other day."

The man looked at her and Winnie shot Mabel a look of warning.

"What did she say?" asked the man, with an air of desperation beneath his coolness.

"Something about Haley getting a job at a, now what do you call them, a new upstart company. Down in California."

"Startup?" asked the man.

"Yes, that's it. A friend of a friend. She got a lucky break."

"Do you know the name of it? Or the city in California?"

"Why are you so interested?"

"I knew Haley years ago. I've got a better job offer for her than anyone else, I'm sure."

Mabel sipped her water. Not likely. The man was a predator, but not a competent one. She'd met a few during her years.

Mabel said, "Haley's mom didn't know the name of the company. And I can't remember what city in California. Los Angeles? San Francisco? I don't know. One of the big cities."

"Do you have her mom's phone number? It's really important."

Eddy brought out Winnie's burger and shake.

"It won't do you any good," said Mabel. "She left yesterday on a Caribbean Cruise. Won it in a contest. She doesn't have one of those cell phones."

The man nodded and said, "Thanks." He went out the door.

Mabel bit into her cheeseburger, tasting the perfect combination of gooey, melted cheddar, grass fed beef, mustard, mayonnaise, lettuce, tomato and whole wheat bun. It was glorious. She momentarily closed her eyes in bliss.

She opened them in time to see Winnie rush to the front door, put up the closed sign and lock the door.

She looked at Mabel.

"You have an amazing talent for deceit. You know that? What's your secret?"

"Yes, I am good. No one suspects an old retired schoolteacher. I've had so much experience ferreting out lies."

HALEY FINISHED THE WHISKEY AS SHE HELD TRIXIE, HER throat burning. Finally, her daughter calmed a bit. Mom went out to the kitchen and brought back a cup of hot chocolate. Trixie went back to her own chair and sipped it.

"I don't know what to do anymore," said Haley. "I'm so tired of running."

"Stop running," said Mom. "I don't know what it'll take to deal with him, but it has to stop. You've got friends and family here to protect you. I'll call the Sheriff. Not that they'll do much good. They're over in Helena and I know they cruise through town periodically, but we can't count on them."

"I'll get a description from Winnie," said Sam. "You'll need to see if you can find a photo online," he looked at her.

Haley nodded.

"You and Trixie are not to leave the ranch alone. Or go riding or walking alone," said Mom. "If you see this guy, either of you, I want you to scream bloody murder. We'll come running. Can you do that?" she asked, looking at Trixie.

Trixie nodded.

"Maybe this afternoon, we should go out into the paddock

and practice while we play with the foals. You need to be loud," said Sam. "It would do them some good to hear yelling. That way they'll get used to it when they're young."

Trixie nodded.

"What should I do?" asked Haley, feeling helpless.

"You find the photo, then get my new computer up and running. It'll take your mind off things," said Mom. "You said you were still trying to find a good way to make reservations. Work on that."

Haley nodded. It was as good an idea as anything. She felt drained. And sort of numb.

The others went into the kitchen. Sam to eat the late lunch he'd bought at Winnie's, Mom to call the Sheriff and work on dinner. Trixie sat at the table finishing up her hot chocolate, looking younger than twelve. Haley hugged her.

"We'll get past this sweet pea. I promise."

Trixie smiled up at her, trustingly.

Haley hugged her again and went to get her laptop. First she looked up James' profile online. The latest photo she found was a couple years old. He had short hair and intentional stubble. He'd started his own tech company. It was still alive. So what was he doing out here?

She went back to her room and hauled in first the printer in its box and then Mom's new computer. She unboxed the printer and set it up to connect with her laptop. Then she took some paper off one of shelves and printed out several copies of James' photo and walked into the kitchen. Haley handed the photos to Sam and Mom.

"Thanks," said Mom. "The Sheriff will be by in a couple of hours. He's in town working on something."

Haley nodded. She went back to the office and unpacked the computer box. Plugged it in and began to set everything up.

She was deep in the process of updating it when Mom called in, "Dinner."

Haley joined Mom, Trixie, Jerry, Dani, Sam and the eight guests. The dining room table was maxed out with that many people. A larger table was something to consider.

The table was covered with a white lace tablecloth. A vase of fresh flowers sat in the center. Greenhouse daisies and lilies. The white and pink lilies still smelled sweet, but were completely overpowered by the scent of Mom's spaghetti.

One of the guests, Ed, had asked about the Bob Marshall Wilderness and Jerry was talking about the hiking trails and the hunting and fishing. The wilderness area was about an hour's drive from Mom's.

"Do you lead trail rides there?" asked his wife.

"Naw, we don't have a license to take people there. It's a ways off for us and we need to stay closer to the ranch. But there are lots of folks who do. You can get phone numbers from one of the ranger stations," said Jerry.

Haley had finished half of her spaghetti when the Sheriff showed up. Mom invited him to dinner and he was pleased to join in. There weren't that many places open in the evening to grab a quick bite to eat.

His name was George Allen and Haley didn't think a more ordinary looking man could be found. Maybe in his fifties, he had brown hair, brown eyes, was an average height, average build. He wasn't macho, like a lot of guys out here. He wasn't wussy either. He just was forgettable, except for his badge. He ate in silence, listening to the conversation of the guests.

Haley hadn't had Mom's spaghetti since the last time she'd been back home. The red sauce with ground beef tasted as good as it ever had. Garlic, onions, basil and Worcestershire sauce. Topped with freshly grated parmesan. The long slinky noodles slipped through her mouth. The red wine, on top of the whiskey she'd had earlier was making her feel a bit tipsy. Which felt nice. She rarely drank and it felt nice to let go a little.

Mom had made an old fashioned chocolate layer cake for one of the guests, who was celebrating her sixty-first birthday. Mom had made fancy flowers with the chocolate frosting. Haley hadn't known she could do that. Mom never ceased to amaze her with the depth of her skills.

After dinner, the guests drove into town. One of the bars was having a swing band play and they'd decided to go dancing.

After they left, Mom and Haley cleared the table and poured coffee. Trixie headed to her room to play with her phone. As Trixie passed the kitchen, Haley heard Trixie pat her leg and click her tongue at Twink and Trouble, who raced down the hall after her.

The Sheriff pushed out his chair and said, "Thanks for the meal Bea. I don't get to eat home cooked meals like that much anymore. It's fast food for me far too often."

"Glad it worked out that way George."

"So, what seems to be the problem?"

Mom filled him in on some of the details and handed him one of the photos of James.

George sat in silence for a few minutes and said, "I don't know how to say this. Personally, I understand this type of thing. The guy's a creep, a stalker and dangerous. The law will say that he hasn't hurt you in nine years and that was in another state. They won't give you a restraining order unless he actually does something violent towards you. It's not right, but there's nothing we can do about it. If I see him hanging around, I can lean a little. Ask him what he's doing here, that sort of thing. I'm not sure that'll do anything for you. He seems determined to find you if he's come all this way. I doubt our attention will have any impact. But, I'll pass the photo around to all the officers who cover this area and they can do the same thing. We can call you and let you know if we see him and where, as a personal favor. But legally, unless he commits a crime, here and now, we're stuck."

Haley hadn't really expected anything.

"So what do I do if he shows up?"

"Call us immediately. We can give him a good talking to. If you tell him to leave and he doesn't, that's another matter. Mostly, if I were you, I'd be careful about when and where you're out in public. And don't be there alone or with just your daughter. Does he have a gun?"

"I have no idea," Haley said.

"If he's served time in Washington and is carrying a gun, even with a permit, we can pick him up. Anyone who's committed a violent misdemeanor or felony, those folks can't have guns."

"Well, if he pulls a gun on me, I guess you'll know," she said.

The Sheriff stared at her. "Do you know how to use a gun."

"Dad taught me, when I was a kid. I don't think I could hit anything though. And I don't want to carry one around with me. I don't want that responsibility. I can't, ..."

"I understand," he said. "Many people don't give it that much thought. Fear takes over and they want a gun. You're very brave."

"Well, I've got a gun and a permit. If that bastard comes near us, I'll shoot him," said Mom.

"Now Bea, he has to actually be threatening your life," George said.

"No, he doesn't. To take that slime's life, I'll go to prison."

"Mom!"

"Now Bea. I've known you a long time. We all want to protect our kids, but you'll do her no good in prison. Your granddaughter either."

"I will if he's dead."

"But what if you missed? What if he still lived? You'd be in prison."

"I won't miss," said Mom, clenching her jaw.

Her reaction made Haley nervous.

"Bea, I have officers who put in twenty, sometimes thirty hours a week doing target practice. They have for years. They're fairly accurate, but not a hundred percent. No one is. Ever."

Mom sighed. "It's just so unfair."

The Sheriff said, "I know it is. Life is unfair. I don't understand why good people die and scum get to live. I never have and I probably never will. We all just do the best we can with the cards that are dealt us. I don't want you to shoot unless he fires first. Got that?"

Mom sat silent for a few minutes, then nodded. Haley wasn't sure Mom had actually acquiesced or not.

"Maybe Trixie and I should leave. Go somewhere else."

George said, "What would that solve? Seems like you been running for nine years. You got a girl who's afraid, won't talk and you destroyed your career because you're always on the run. I don't think confrontations are always the right answer either, but running hasn't worked in this situation."

Sam, who'd been silent the entire time, said, "He's right. Leaving is a bad idea. You've been trying to fight this by yourself for nine years. Time to try another tactic."

"What?" said Haley. "I have no more ideas."

"He's a city boy you said. Well, let's scare him. This is a small town. We'll get everyone involved."

"What did you have in mind?" asked George.

"Doesn't Frank have that wolf he trained?"

"Frank Helmsman? Don't think he's a real joiner," said the Sheriff.

"But he likes Bea. She took him in last year when he flooded out. Everybody likes Bea."

Sheriff Allen looked thoughtful. "First you'll have to find out where he's staying," he said.

"I thought I'd swing into town early tomorrow. Take some of these photos around, so people can start being unfriendly," said Sam.

They continued discussing ideas until the Sheriff had to leave. He lived in Helena and still had an hour's drive to get home. Sam left at the same time, promising to come back tomorrow to work with the foals.

Haley felt a little calmer. She worked longer on getting the new computer up and running. Finally, at 11 p.m. she called it a night.

The guests had their own key and would probably be coming in late. She had to be up around seven in the morning to help Mom. Mom would be up around five.

Before going to bed, Haley stopped in Trixie's room and hugged her. Trixie was in bed reading. She was weighed down by Trouble and Twinkletoes, curled up on either side of her.

"You're spoiling them, Mom says."

Trixie smiled.

"Guess you've needed some animals around you. I'm sorry, it never occurred to me that you'd like a pet."

Trixie shrugged, as if to say it wasn't important.

"I love you dear. I want you to spend time enjoying your life."

Trixie picked up her phone and typed in 'Love you too' with a flashing red heart next to it.

Haley hugged her and said, "Lights out, phone away," and went to bed.

How safe would Trixie have to feel before she'd talk again? Would she ever talk again?

CHAPTER 14 ~ MABEL

MABEL WAS AT THE GROCERY STORE IN LINCOLN THE NEXT day, in their tiny produce department. She picked up each lemon, trying to find one ripe enough to have a scent. She wasn't succeeding. They all smelled waxy. The mushrooms next to them had more scent, that earthy, musty smell.

Why did she bother? She should just stop cooking. But she'd found a recipe for lemon chicken in a magazine and was intrigued enough to try it.

Sheriff Allen appeared, holding a soda in one hand and a muffin in the other. He looked distracted.

"Mabel, could I have a word?"

Her heart leapt into her throat.

"Certainly Sheriff." If he was shopping for snacks, would he arrest her?

"Winnie told me you talked to that fella who's looking for Haley."

"Yes, I did." Was that what this was about? Not the robberies? She took a deep breath and let it out slowly.

"She says you steered him in the wrong direction?"

"I sure hope so. I didn't like the looks of him."

"Good for you. Had you seen him around before or since."

"No, I haven't."

"Well, if you do, let me know, okay. You don't have to talk to him. Just call me," he said, handing her his business card. "Leave a detailed message if I don't answer."

"I'll be sure to do that," she said, taking his card and putting it in her purse. "Do you think he'll cause trouble?"

"I don't know. I suspect he will if he finds her. She thinks he will."

"Well, her word's enough for me. She was always truthful. I've always liked that gal."

"Well, I've gotta get back on the road. Times a' wastin'."

"Drive carefully," she said.

"Thanks Mabel. I wish everyone around here was like you. Then I'd be out of a job. That would be a good thing."

She laughed. Little did he know.

He was a kind soul. Brightened her day.

She finished her grocery shopping and drove home.

She had two more baby blankets to make. Then she'd drive over to Helena and drop them off at the hospital. They always needed baby blankets, for the newborns or for babies in the hospital. Maybe she could talk Winnie into taking half a day off after finishing her baking. Or maybe Bea. Even better would be both. They could make a day of it.

Haley's alarm didn't go off the next morning. She woke up feeling drugged and exhausted, like she'd tossed and turned the whole night. Which she had.

What really woke her up was the smell of breakfast sausage cooking. She looked at the clock and it said 9:28 a.m. An hour and a half late.

"Crap." She rolled out of bed and went to the dresser. Pulled out some clean underwear, socks and jeans. Then to a t-shirt. Time to do laundry again.

After dressing she ran the brush through her hair and sipped water from the glass on her bedside table. She put some lotion on her face, hands and elbows. She'd have to wash her face later. The guests were probably up and using the bathroom.

Mom really needed to build another bathroom.

She went past Trixie's door. It was closed. She might be awake or still asleep. Haley went into the kitchen. Mom was at the stove, cooking eggs as well as the sausages.

Haley's stomach rumbled at the smell.

"Why didn't you wake me? Sorry, my alarm didn't go off. I can't remember if I set it or not."

"I decided you needed the sleep."

Haley poured a cup of coffee. She sipped the rich, bitter liquid and savored it.

"What do you want me to do?"

"You can keep the toast going," said Mom.

Haley took the already popped up toast from the toaster and put in four more slices of bread for the next round. She buttered the toasted bread, adding to the stack on a serving plate.

Three of the guests were already at the dining room table, so Haley took the plate out for them to get started on.

"Good morning," she said.

"Good morning," they replied.

"Do you need more coffee? Or water? Or juice?"

"We're doing fine," said the woman.

Haley couldn't remember her name. She returned to the kitchen and started loading up more toast.

"The sausages are ready," said Mom, who was still working on eggs.

"Trixie up yet?"

"I haven't seen her. She went to bed pretty late last night didn't she?"

"She was going bed with Twink and Trouble."

"They are madly in love with her," said Mom. "It's good to see. I think she needs some animals around her. You always did."

"Did I?"

"You were always happier with them."

"I don't remember."

Why hadn't she had animals in Seattle? Before life got disrupted. Probably too many late hours and long days at work. She was never at home. Hadn't been during college either. Then after they'd left James, they always needed to move at a moment's notice. It wasn't as easy to find an apartment if you had pets.

The morning passed quickly with the normal laundry and other cleaning chores. Around one, Sam arrived to work with the foals.

Haley was out in back, hanging up laundry by the vegetable garden and saw him talking to Mom, while he waited for Trixie to get the halters and lead ropes.

Haley continued to hang sheets out on the line. They didn't dry quickly in the cold, but there was wind, and the sheets would eventually dry. They would smell better than if they'd been dried in the dryer, plus save on the electric bill. Always a bonus.

Mom came back to the house to start working on dinner.

"What did Sam have to say?" asked Haley.

Mom stopped and looked at her.

"How much of this do you want to know? I don't want to worry you."

"I think I need to be kept in the loop."

"He's still in town. Staying at Fischer's Motel. Sam asked them to suddenly be full up with reservations come the weekend, but apparently James has reserved a room for the next two weeks. So he asked them to be unfriendly. Lorna said she'd work on that. We're moving to Plan B."

"Which is what?"

"I'm going to call Frank Helmsman. See if he'll do me a favor."

Haley nodded.

"What can I do?"

"You're already helping. Maybe find some time to work on websites? Tourist season is coming up for both Winnie and us. And I believe Sam's a paying customer."

"But you need help too."

"So get me more paying customers. I'll need to hire more

help for the summer. The sooner I can pay them, the better," said Mom. "And I've got a hot tub to buy, right? That sure would feel nice on my achy old bones."

Haley nodded. "I'm on it."

She spent the rest of the afternoon getting the reservation system up and running. She'd finally found one that worked. Then she took out a few ads for Mom in the local tourist magazines. She added the final touches to Winnie's website. Both of them were up and running, just humming along. She had her mojo back. Tomorrow, she'd tackle Sam's website.

Haley called Winnie to let her know the progress, so she could plan on hiring a couple more people. Haley suggested a couple of websites to take online ads out on and gave Winnie prices.

By the time she finished the call, the smells of dinner were rolling in beneath her closed door. Chili and home baked cornbread. Mom had also made chocolate pudding cake earlier in the day. Haley suggested she rename it chocolate molten lava cake. Which she did.

Haley had gotten a chalkboard for the dining room. At the end of every meal Trixie wrote the menu for the next meal on it. She had lovely writing and an eye for making the menu look interesting, adding beautiful colored designs around the edges. The guests loved being able to see the menu in advance so they could plan whether to eat at the ranch or elsewhere. Mostly, they chose to eat at the ranch. Lunch and dinner were extra, but the cost was moderate and the food reliably good.

After dinner, the guests turned the tv on in the entertainment room to watch the news. The weather wasn't looking good. The chinook had started the snow melting and torrential rain was forecast for most days this week. That would bring the river level up even higher.

Mom looked worried. She was writing instructions on her

notepad of things to talk about with Jerry and Dani in the morning.

The next day after breakfast Mom told Haley to go back to her room and work online. So she went to work on Sam's website. It really was awful. The original designer had made a mess of it. The only thing to do was start over. She emailed Sam that she was taking it down for a few days.

By lunch, clam chowder, she'd gotten some of the bones finished. She sat at the table with the guests and the ranch staff. Everyone was happy to be inside out of the deluge. The guests always seemed to enjoy talking to Dani and Jerry, finding out what it was like working on a small ranch.

"Is Sam coming over to work with the foals?" asked Haley.

"No, he called to say one of his mares is about to have her first foal. He's sticking close to home until she foals," said Mom.

Trixie didn't look disappointed to stay inside. She was deep into a series of books and all she wanted to do was read.

"This clam chowder hits the spot," said one of the guests. "I would never have thought of adding bacon to mine. Thanks for the idea."

"Thank you, I learned that trick from my mother," said Mom, "and I thought we needed some warmth today."

"I sure do," said Dani. "We got all the cows moved up to the house pasture, farther from the river and the lowlands. It's really wet out there."

"Good, I'm glad you got that done. I rode out this morning. The river's really high. They're expecting flooding. I want to keep all the livestock close by," said Mom.

"Will it flood this high up?" asked Dani.

"It has before," said Mom. She looked at the guests. "The house has always been safe. But some of the pastures are on lower ground and much closer to the river. Those are at risk."

They nodded at her. They were sort of local, from Billings.

None of them were retired and seemed just happy to just sit back and relax: to read, watch tv, play cards and eat good food. To be taken care of. Theresa, a local massage therapist, was coming out today to give massages to people in their rooms. That ought to make them very happy.

Hell, that would make her happy. It would be great to build on a dedicated room for massages. Have Theresa out here full time in the busy months. Haley had lots of dreams.

She was spending the day building Sam's website. Which was entertaining her. She felt sore and stiff though. A hot shower would be the best she could hope for. Or maybe she could talk Dani into using her bath tub, out in her cabin. Mom really needed to build another bathroom in the house.

The rain went on and the river rose.

A day later Haley rode out with Mom to look at things. The ground was saturated enough that puddles weren't going away. That happened in Seattle all the time. Not here in Montana. The soil here usually absorbed as much as it could get.

The air smelled fresh. The saddle was soaked where her rain poncho wasn't covering it. The bay mare's fur looked black from the moisture, but she plodded on through the squelchy mud.

Haley tilted her head back and drank some rain to moisten her dry mouth. The rain felt cold. It was only forty degrees. Just warm enough to melt the snow. Haley's long underwear wasn't cutting it. She was grateful for the gloves, but her exposed face felt like ice.

The river was coming over the banks, drowning the evacuated cattle pasture. Haley could see the fencing, more than half underwater. Not just a foot, but nearly three feet of water stood over the grass.

Mom was shaking her head.

The river ran white and frothy. Large chunks of ice, not yet melted, moved downstream with the rushing current. As did trees taken down by the flooding upstream. One hit a corner of the fence, taking rails with it.

When the pasture dried out there would be a lot of work to do before they could put cattle back on it.

The sound was deafening. The river roared down its main channel, carving out more territory as it went.

A huge structure, wood and steel, surfed the waves. Tossed against the fence. Took out more rails. Then it was gone, taken down the river.

Haley was shocked at the violence of it. The mare twitched, jumpy. Both of them wanted to get out of there.

Mom yelled, "There went the Meyer's bridge. They're stuck over there until they can get a new one built."

Haley knew they Meyers. They'd lived here when she was a kid. This wasn't the first time they'd lost a bridge. They would have stocked up on food and supplies. Still, it was an awful thing. That bridge must have been expensive to build.

They watched for a few more minutes, before Mom urged her horse on.

They rode on a trail around the near end of the pasture. The far end was underwater, perhaps gone, taken by the river. The pasture had lost a lot of ground. And this wasn't even the peak yet. There was still plenty of snow to melt. How high would the river go this year?

CHAPTER 16 ~ MABEL

MABEL CLOSED THE FRONT DOOR OF HER HOUSE AND HEFTED the green cloth bag of paperback books over her shoulder. She wore her light spring coat today and her walking shoes. A pair of plain brown oxfords, navy pants and a light blue blouse. The sun was out and it had stopped raining for a bit.

As she walked down the steps, Mabel admired her daffodils. She loved their yellow cheeriness. Brightening up a spring day, they gave her feelings of hope that summer would be coming soon. She smiled and walked closer to them, their slight scent refreshed the air. They showed up every year. She didn't fertilize them or do any of the things people said one should do. She just admired them. And occasionally, pulled a few weeds. A gardener, she was not.

She walked down the street to the highway and then headed East. The air was warm, nearly sixty degrees. The temperatures had jumped twenty degrees in a day. Maybe the climate was changing like everyone said. The Blackfoot River was running higher than normal, a couple weeks earlier than usual. She supposed she'd get used to it. Humans were adaptable.

Nature would adapt too, but there would be a lot of loss first. So many species wouldn't survive.

She walked quickly, for her. The warm breeze brushed her face. There wasn't much traffic on the highway this morning. It was a weekday and tourist season wouldn't begin for another month. She strode beside the highway. There was a wide gravel area, mostly used by truckers or camping trailers, pulling over to park and grab something to eat, or shop. The space was nearly always empty, like today. The highway was rarely busy even in summer, never in winter. Most people used the four lane highway over by Helena these days. Roger's Pass could be dangerous in summer, in winter it was treacherous.

Mabel smiled. She missed teaching at this time of year. Even though it was always harder. All the kids getting spring fever, anticipating school ending in about a month. But their energy was so wonderful. It was contagious. And she loved summer vacation too.

She heard yelling and turned to look across the highway. In front of Fischer's bright yellow Motel stood that man from the other day. Haley's ex. He was yelling at Frank Helmsman's black wolf. Frank was hiding around the corner of the Motel, not visible to the man. He saw Mabel and put his finger to his mouth in a shh motion.

Frank's wolf, Shadow, was simply walking towards the man.

"Help, help me, someone! Wolf! Stay away from me. You go away." The man scrambled into his car and locked the door, then drove quickly away. Mabel could see the shocked look on his pinched white face.

Shadow just plopped down on the sidewalk, looking injured.

Mabel knew Shadow. While he looked intimidating, wolves rarely attacked people. Especially, well fed, well socialized wolves like Shadow.

He'd been found as a baby, his mother killed by a car, his siblings died. Shadow had been the only survivor and Frank took the tiny thing home and raised him, feeding him by hand until he was old enough to eat on his own. The wolf was just as affectionate as any dog. Although he was very large. People had such peculiar ideas about wolves and that man clearly knew nothing about them.

She turned away and continued her walk. Interesting that Frank had turned Shadow loose on the man. What was he up to? When she got home, Mable would call the sheriff and tell him that she'd seen the man.

Mabel waved at Winnie as she walked through the wide parking area in front the cafe. Winnie was standing outside, staring at her empty flower boxes. The weather had everybody thinking about summer.

With the season getting warmer, Mabel wouldn't have many more chances to wear a coat and scarf, her disguise. And a dirty, muddy car with an obscured license plate.

When she opened the door to the library, Mabel figured she had time to get one more robbery done.

She better get planning.

CHAPTER 17 ~ HALEY

HALEY SAT AT THE TABLE IN HER ROOM, DRINKING ANOTHER cup of coffee. She'd grown to love this room. A fragrant bunch of lilacs sat in a blue vase on the table, their perfume filling the room. Her quiet oasis amidst the chaos of all the guests and life with her Mom and Trixie and the ranch hands trooping in and out. She could get her work done here, mostly without interruption.

She opened the old wooden cigar box on top of the table and took out a cloth, dusting off the laptop screen. Then returned it to the box.

She'd finished up work on Sam's website. It was one of the best she'd ever done. She shot off an email with the link so he could take a look at it. Haley leaned back in her chair, taking another sip of coffee.

Since Mom's and Winnie's websites had gone live, she'd had three more people come forward, looking for help with theirs. The motel, one of the restaurants and an outfitting company. It felt good to have paying jobs lined up. She could put some money into savings.

"Haley," said Mom, rapping on the door.

"Come in," she said.

Mom opened the door and said, "I can't find Trixie."

"Where is she supposed to be?" asked Haley, checking the time.

"She's supposed to be setting the table for lunch."

"You checked the usual places, her room, the chickens, the horses?"

"Yes, of course."

"I'll go find her," said Haley. "Sorry, she's usually good about doing her work."

She texted Trixie. There was no response, but Haley heard Trixie's phone pinging down the hall. She got up and went into Trixie's room. She texted again. The pinging came from the window ledge. Trixie's phone sat there, plugged in to charge.

"Well, that's not helpful. She must be using her notepad to talk to people."

Mom stood behind her. A worried expression on her face.

"I'll go outside and look around, ask people."

"Don't go far by your self," said Mom.

"I won't."

Haley went back into her room and pulled her boots on. Then grabbed a sweater. She checked the chicken coop again. And the barn. Found Twinkletoes lounging on a plastic covered bale of bedding. The cat chirruped at her. She swore the cat had gotten fatter and lazier since she and Trixie had arrived.

"Where's your friend Trixie gotten to?" Haley asked, rubbing the cat's head.

She called, but Trixie didn't appear. Trouble wasn't around either.

She went into the horse pasture. The mares and geldings were grazing and the foals were stretched out sleeping in the sun.

Haley checked the house pasture where the cattle had been

moved to, but Trixie wasn't there either. She yelled and yelled, but Trixie didn't appear.

By then, she was beginning to panic. If Trixie was stuck somewhere or fallen and hurt, she probably wouldn't, maybe even couldn't, yell out. Even if she did there might not be anyone close enough to hear. Why had she left the house without her phone? They would have to talk about that.

Haley walked down to the river, calling. The water had come up even more. It had swallowed the south and big pine pastures.

She took her phone out and called the house.

"Mom, is Trixie back yet?"

"No honey. Come back up to the house. Then, all of us will take horses and go on an organized search for her."

"But there might not be time. What if she's in danger?"

"It'll be better if all of us are out searching. Now come back here."

"Okay," said Haley, grudgingly.

Her mother, the voice of reason. She headed back towards the house. A huge roar came from behind her.

A huge group of pines, fencing and presumably the land beneath had been taken by the turbulent waters. Sixty foot tall trees were tossed around in the river. The sound was deafening. The power of the Blackfoot and its churning waters terrified her.

"Trixie please don't be anywhere near the river," Haley said.

Then she turned back and ran towards the house. Mom was right. They all needed to be searching. She couldn't do it alone.

She ran about halfway there, then had to slow down. The muscles in her legs burned and she couldn't catch her breath. She used to be able to run all the way between the house and the river. She was out of shape. Then again she used to run in sneakers, not cowboy boots.

Haley went as fast as she could the rest of the way, trying to think about anything but Trixie. It didn't work. It was sort of like trying to meditate. Whenever she thought of something else, worries about Trixie would appear.

Trixie was her whole life and Haley had been ignoring her. Why hadn't she checked up on Trixie earlier in the day? Why had she just assumed Trixie was in her room reading.

Because she was too busy working. She didn't really have time to work for Mom for their bed and board, do work on the side to make money so they could get back on their feet, and be a good parent to Trixie. There was not enough time in the day. And she had no time to just relax.

She was a mess and there was no balance in her life. She'd been doing this sort of thing for years. Something had to go. But what?

She'd caught her breath again by the time she got back to the house. Everyone else had finished lunch. The guests had gone for a drive into town.

Dani, Jerry and Mom waited while she downed a cheese sandwich and some iced tea.

They made plans as to who would ride where. Jerry and Dani were going to split up and go through all the cattle pastures and wooded areas between the house and the river.

"Be careful," said Haley. "I just saw a huge clump of pine and pasture drop into the river. A chunk about as large as the house."

Mom shook her head. "That's not good. How far is that damn river going to rise this year? The weather service says it hasn't peaked yet and we're already flooding more than ever before. There's still a lot of snow on the pass left to melt."

Mom and Haley were going to ride together, off towards Sam's.

"Has anyone seen Trouble lately," asked Haley. "I wonder if he's with her."

Mom went out back and yelled for him. The dog didn't

come. Jerry and Dani went out to the barn to start saddling up horses.

Mom wrote a note to Trixie, telling her to call Haley if she got back before they did.

Haley rode a buckskin gelding named Sooty. She liked him, he was a smart, no nonsense kind of horse. He did everything anyone asked of him. All of Mom's horses had a lot of common sense, but he was one of the most reliable. Mom sold the horses that didn't measure up.

They rode out through the woods, yelling every now and then, stopping to listen and look. The sky was dark with rain clouds. That would only increase the flooding.

There was a trail now that led between Mom's house and Sam's, since he'd been coming over almost daily. He'd made a gate in the wire fence, dividing their properties. Mom opened it and rode through, Haley rode through and maneuvered the gelding so she could pull the gate closed and latch it.

They rode through the woods, still yelling for Trixie and startled a small herd of deer.

Haley was becoming more and more anxious.

Trixie just didn't disappear. She had always left a message for Haley when she was going somewhere. But life here at Mom's was different. The ranch was a big place and if her daughter was somewhere on the ranch, maybe Trixie didn't actually consider it going anywhere. But Haley didn't think Trixie would have gone to Sam's without telling someone.

They rode up to the house. Sam's truck was parked in front, but no one answered the door. They tied the horses to the fence and began looking in the outbuildings. The garage was empty. So was the arena.

They looked in the barn and found him washing a colt in the wash rack. The colt looked nervous. He probably never had a bath before. His mother stood cross tied in the hallway nearby, dozing.

"Well, hello ladies. What brings you here?"

"We can't find Trixie. We thought we'd look here."

A worried expression crossed his face.

"How long?"

"Haven't seen her since breakfast," said Mom. She glanced at her watch. "It's two now."

"I saw her this morning. She and your dog were walking at the far end of my property."

"Highway side or river side?" asked Mom.

"River side," said Sam.

"We'd better get down there. Large chunks of our land's been disappearing into the river. Yours probably has too," said Mom.

"I'll come with you. This young 'uns had enough for today."

Sam grabbed a towel and quickly rubbed the colt dry. The little guy obviously enjoyed it, closing his eyes in pleasure. Then Sam unsnapped his halter and led the mother back outside, the colt romping along behind.

He said, "Why don't you turn your horses loose in this paddock for a bit? The trail down by the river isn't really horse ready. It's awfully rocky and there's still too many downed logs. That's part of the ten year plan."

They unsaddled and unbridled the horses, putting the tack on the ground outside of the fence and leaving the horses to graze.

Then followed Sam on a narrow trail that led down towards the river.

He was right, once they had gone past all the pastures, the land was covered with downed trees. They walked along logs, mostly aspen, for most of the way to the river.

Then it opened out onto sagebrush and rocks. Huge jagged rocks, that the river may have tossed around a million years ago when this was riverbed, before the river shifted and chose another path. Or maybe they just rolled down from the mountain on the other side of the river.

Either way, the whole trip was slow going and rough. They yelled. Out from behind one of the massive rocks came Trouble. Barking and barking.

They moved as fast as they could. Behind the rock about twenty feet from the river was Trixie.

It looked like she'd fallen into a hole. Between three boulders. Her forehead bled as if she'd knocked her head on a rock. She was unconscious. The Blackfoot roared in the background.

"Trixie, can you hear me?" asked Haley.

Trixie moaned, didn't open her eyes. Mom was on the phone. Calling an ambulance. Then Jerry and Dani.

Sam and Haley pulled Trixie out of the hole and lay her flat on the ground. Her t-shirt was ripped and her running shoes and shorts dirty, as was her skin.

"I can't tell if she hurt her back or not," said Sam. "I don't want to move her much, until they bring a stretcher."

Trouble sat and whined, worried. Tears ran down Haley's face. She sat down on the hard rocks near Trixie's head.

Trixie's leg, below the knee was clearly broken. Haley could see bone sticking out of the broken skin. She brushed Trixie's face with her hand.

"Honey, it's going to be okay. You stay here with us, okay? We'll get you home safe and sound."

Sam said, "I'll go back to the house, lead them here."

"Would it be any faster to cut through our property? We have a road that goes mostly down to the river," said Mom.

He looked thoughtful and said, "I don't think so. We're the farthest away from your property line that we can get on my ranch. There's too many rocks to go over. Let's hope they're sending young, agile men with the stretcher. Did you describe where we're at?"

Mom nodded.

Sam said, "Maybe we need the search & rescue team. I don't think the ambulance has a backcountry stretcher. I'll call Ian, down the road."

He pulled out his cell and was talking to someone. "Yeah, we need a stretcher, the kind you can tie someone into, and two men who are agile. We're talking about walking on logs and rocky terrain here. She's a young girl. Maybe eighty pounds. Great. I'll be up at the barn to meet you!" He had to yell to be heard.

"Okay, they're on their way. She'll be okay."

"Sam, bring a little water and a clean cloth, okay?" asked Mom. "She's been out here a long time. Let's see if we can get some water into her."

"Will do," he said, going back towards the house.

Haley said, "I should have checked on her earlier."

"Nonsense. This isn't your fault. It's an accident," said Mom, pacing around. "I'm only glad we found her."

"I'm trying to do too much."

"You always have. You've always tried to be everything to everybody. Do you remember when you were her age?"

Haley shook her head.

"You were riding Biscuit, trying to become the best cowhand in the world. Competing in the state spelling bee, trying to read the entire school library, taking dancing lessons and you wanted to join 4-H and raise a foal. You wanted to do everything."

"But then I didn't have a child to take care of."

"I know."

"What should I do?"

"Oh my goodness. I have no idea," said Mom.

"What would you do in my place?"

"I think you should stay here. Help me with the B an B. Let

Trixie grow stronger and put down roots. And in the fall, you should send her back to school. Whether she's talking or not."

"I've thought about that. I just don't know what she needs. Other than to feel safe."

"None of us know what our children need, dear. At least I never did."

Haley closed her eyes. The river roared past them, twenty feet away. All the power in the universe. She could feel the dampness from its spray in the surrounding air. The sky was filled with dark clouds that looked ready to open up and dump rain on them at any minute.

Haley paced back and forth. Her life was a mess and all she could think about was how she'd messed up. She needed to be thinking about her daughter.

What did Trixie need?

CHAPTER 18 ~ MABEL

MABEL PARKED THE BLACK FORD PICKUP IN THE NEAR EMPTY street, just past the glass door of the old drugstore. Pale yellow paint peeled from its outside walls. The air was chilly, but had warmed up a bit from earlier in the day. Things were definitely melting now with all this rain. It was pouring outside.

She tightened the clear plastic rain scarf beneath her chin and pulled it forward a bit. The wig came forward as well. Just a bit. The bangs hung to her eyelashes.

She took a sip of the bitter coffee. It was too strong. She'd get some better coffee later. She set the paper to-go cup back in her cupholder.

Mabel stepped out of the navy pickup and down into the slush of the street. Good thing she had rubber boots on.

The main street was quiet. A few people over at the post office, that was it.

The way she liked it.

She walked into the drugstore and over to look at an aisle with hand lotion. The drugstore smelled of cloying floral perfume. She wrinkled up her nose. Perfume always made her feel sneezy. She chose a pair of sunglasses with large lenses. Ones that covered a good amount of her face.

Cheesy pop music played over the sound system. It grated on her nerves. Some young girl singing about love. The poor thing probably had no idea what real love was.

There was a woman in a navy blouse standing at the pharmacy counter where you checked out. That was it. No one else in the store. The woman looked like one of those no-nonsense types. That wouldn't make it easy.

Mabel walked over to the counter and pulled the gun out of her large purse, making the usual demand.

The woman glared at her, but did as she asked. Even gave her the money under the drawer without Mabel having to ask.

"Why are you doing this?" she asked.

"I need the money," said Mabel. "At my age I'm not into thrills."

She took the plastic bag of money and walked out the front door hurriedly. Back into the pickup and drove off. She drove into Billings, pulled into the busy drive-through at a coffee shop. Removed the rain scarf, fake glasses and wig. Peeled the price tag off the sunglasses. Then wiggled out of her coat and tossed everything in the small space behind her bench seat and the wall of the pickup cab.

It wasn't until she was halfway home that Mabel realized what was bothering her. She hadn't consciously checked the drugstore for cameras before the robbery.

And she'd seen one, but the camera hadn't registered until now. Right behind the cashier and taking in a view of the the counter in front of the cash register. And Mabel.

Mabel had been so focused on the robbery it had just now dawned on her.

She could only hope there wasn't one outside the store that got her car license. Maybe it had been raining too hard.

CHAPTER 19 ~ HALEY

Haley rode in the ambulance with Trixie. It had an antiseptic, clean smell about it. The scent was as close to the hospital smell as one could get in a vehicle she supposed. She hated it.

The weather was warm, so she'd taken her coat off and was sitting down, leaning against the hard, uncomfortable wall, while the medical guy checked Trixie's vitals. Haley didn't know if he was a nurse, doctor or if he had another title.

Trixie's face was pale and she was still unconscious.

Haley held Trixie's hand and with her free hand held the water bottle Sam had brought back from the house. She sipped the cool water, then closed the top with her mouth.

The long trip to Helena seemed to take forever, even though it was only about an hour and a quarter.

Mom was going to contact her guests and have them eat dinner out. Dani had volunteered to cook breakfast. So Mom would get the car and drive to the hospital in Helena. She'd also bring Haley's purse and Trixie's phone.

Haley felt numb. She was coping fairly well given the

119

circumstances. The long ride gave her plenty of time to list her failures as a parent.

About halfway to Helena, Trixie became conscious. She opened her eyes.

"How are you feeling?" asked the medical guy, whose badge read Xavier.

Trixie nodded her head.

"Does your head hurt?" asked Haley.

Trixie nodded and pointed to the side of her head, where blood matted her hair.

"Does anywhere else hurt, other than your leg?" asked the medic.

Trixie looked thoughtful for a minute and then shook her head.

At the hospital, Trixie was admitted immediately. Haley spent her time filling out form after form in the emergency room with Trixie, thankful she had health insurance, although she hadn't brought any of her information. It was in her purse that Mom was bringing.

The white walls of the emergency room triage area looked newly painted, clean and well taken care of. They were accented with blond wood or faux wood panes. She was going to spend a long time looking at them.

Haley sat in a brown plastic chair. After she'd finished the forms, she watched the emergency doc, who'd introduced herself as Dr. Elizabeth Tanner. The tall, horsey looking woman went about her work methodically, checking for other injuries beyond the obvious one. The ambulance crew hadn't done much other than given Trixie an over the counter painkiller and clean the wound.

The doctor asked Trixie, "How do you feel?"

"She doesn't talk," said Haley.

"What do you mean?" asked the doctor.

"A few years ago, she witnessed the murder of the woman who cared for her when I was at work. She hasn't spoken since."

"Does she communicate with you?"

"Yes, she writes notes or texts."

A nurse came in and wheeled Trixie down the hall for x-rays.

"It won't take long," said Dr. Tanner. "Then we'll know exactly what we're dealing with."

Haley hadn't realized how tired she was. Her phone said it was after six and her stomach rumbled with emptiness. She didn't care. She just wanted Trixie to be all right.

A nurse came to the door, she and the doc conferred.

Then Dr. Tanner said to Haley, "We need this room for another emergency patient. I'm going to have you move out to the waiting room until we get Trixie's x-rays back. I'll let you know as soon as we find anything out.

Haley sat out in the waiting room and waited. The walls were also white with blond wood accents. There were a lot of windows, leaving the place feeling light and airy. Two aquariums filled with colorful fish stood on top of tall stands at each end of the waiting area. Haley watched the fish. They were calming and relaxing to watch as they moved through the water and around and through the fake coral reefs. Hypnotic. Which was probably why they were there.

Finally, Mom arrived. She gave Haley her purse and a bag of takeout food. They ate the rubbery burgers with too much mustard. Then Haley remembered to give the receptionist her insurance information. She and Mom waited. Eventually, Dr. Tanner came out.

The doctor said, "She had a pretty severe bang to the head. We'll need to keep her here overnight, maybe two nights, depending on how that head injury is doing. We've moved her to a hospital room. We've set her leg, it's a clean break, so that's good. It should grow back just fine. But I don't want her wobbling around on crutches with a head injury. You know teenagers, they think they're invincible," she smiled.

"Thank you," said Haley.

"Has she ever gotten therapy for not speaking?"

"Whenever we could afford it, yes. For years. They've all just said, she'll talk when she feels safe enough."

The doctor nodded and led them to the front desk, then disappeared back into the corridor she'd come from.

A nurse at the desk gave them Haley's room number and pointed them in the direction of the elevators.

They took the elevator up to the third floor and found Trixie's room. The whole hospital looked new, although Haley knew it wasn't. Fresh paint in a cheery green color, not the awful sea green she remembered from some hospital of her childhood.

Trixie's room was airy and spacious for a hospital room. She had it to herself. The window looked out onto the city. Her room was painted a warm blue color, almost turquoise.

Trixie was sitting up, drinking from a plastic water bottle with a straw. Her color looked much better. She put the bottle down on the tray table at her side when she saw them.

Haley hugged her and Trixie hugged back, not letting go.

"I'm so glad you're okay, honey," said Haley, tears leaking out the corners of her eyes. She wiped her face.

"Mom," Trixie said quietly. Her voice came out in a croak.

Haley looked at her.

Trixie said, "I'm sorry I left without telling you. It was stupid."

Trixie slurred her words slightly.

Haley's Mom said, "You sure had us scared," as if Trixie's talking was a normal thing.

Haley decided it probably was best not to make a big deal out of it. She didn't want Trixie to stop talking.

"Well, I guess you won't be doing that again," said Haley.

"Mom's right, we were so afraid. We had no idea where you were, but I'm glad that you're okay. How do you feel?"

Trixie said, "My head hurts."

"Not your leg?" asked Haley.

"Not yet."

"Are you hungry?" asked Mom.

Trixie nodded.

Haley went to the nurse's station. Two nurses were there, entering information into computers.

"My daughter was just brought in. She hasn't eaten since breakfast this morning. I wonder if it's possible to get her some food. Or do I need to go out to a restaurant and bring something back?"

"Let me call the kitchen, see if they can rustle something up for her," said one of the nurses.

"Thank you. I'll be in her room."

Haley went back inside and sat down again. Her heart felt like it would melt with relief. Trixie was going to be all right.

Mom and Trixie were talking about Trouble.

"He wouldn't leave me. He just stayed beside me to protect me. I know I was unconscious, but I could feel him there."

"He's a good dog," Mom said.

"How are the chicks?"

Haley marveled at the miracle of her daughter speaking again. She wanted to cry, but held it back.

So, she sat and listened to Trixie and Mom talk, reveling in their conversation.

And tried to figure out how to get her life together.

CHAPTER 20 ~ MABEL

M ABEL STOOD IN HER KITCHEN, WAITING FOR THE COFFEE TO finish brewing. She'd washed all her dishes with lemony dish soap, wiped down the tan formica counters and the wooden kitchen table.

The small kitchen tv sat on the counter. She had the morning news on, listening for any reference to her. Finally, she heard it.

"And now fresh news on the so-called *Granny Bandit*. She robbed a drugstore in the Billings area yesterday. And this time she was caught on tape."

Mabel watched in horror as the black and white footage showed her waving her gun at the woman and then taking the bag of money. There was no sound.

It didn't look like her. And if she'd hadn't known better, Mabel wouldn't have really believed it was an old woman. Except that she walked slowly. The long wig and sunglasses hid most of her face. But the mouth area was wrinkled and jowly. That part definitely looked old.

She plopped down at the kitchen table, staring at the tv.

"Reports are that she drove a navy pickup, but we don't

have a make, model or license plate number. So if your granny drives a blue pickup, make sure you know where she's at," said the commentator, laughing.

Mabel turned the tv off. She was glad the newscaster treated the robbery as a joke. She was sure the police weren't.

This time she'd stolen $14,964.38. More than ever before. That was it. She wouldn't do it again. Her life of crime was over.

This afternoon, she'd clean and switch the license plates back to her main car, the dark green Subaru wagon. And she'd hose down the pickup till it was spotless and looked like it hadn't seen mud, ever. Just in case the police hadn't told the tv stations everything they knew.

Mabel got up and poured a cup of coffee. Then went into the living room, turned on the big tv and clicked through the channels until she found a good movie.

An old musical with Gene Kelly and Frank Sinatra. Mabel sat down and began crocheting, the pale yellow yarn sliding through her fingers as she quickly worked it. She was making a yellow and white baby blanket for the hospital. Once a month she took a bunch of them over to the hospital in Helena, for the newborns.

She stopped and sipped her coffee, savoring the warmth. She felt cold today for some reason, even though the weather was getting warmer every day. Moving closer to summer and the days were getting longer.

She needed to get out of the house. To be around other people more. Her brain was rattling around inside her skull and making her nervous.

She put her crocheting away in the basket beneath the coffee table and turned off the tv. Then called Bea, but there was no answer, which was unusual. She didn't leave a message.

She glanced at her watch. Well, it was almost lunchtime.

She'd wander on over to Winnie's. Take herself out to lunch. And after that, clean up the cars and the garage.

Mabel stuck her cup of coffee in the fridge. She'd put it in the microwave later.

She slipped into her lavender coat, it was about the right warmth, and stuck her wallet in the pocket, then zipped it up. She checked her hair in the hallway mirror. It was wild as usual. Not much she could do about that, but she patted it anyway.

She opened the door and noticed it was raining, so Mabel grabbed a hat and went outside.

She locked the house up and put her keys in the empty pocket on the other side, so she felt balanced.

Mabel walked quickly to Winnie's where the line reached out the door. People were standing in the rain, waiting for a table at Winnie's. Now that was different.

She stopped and looked at the line, her mouth open wide. Nothing to do, but stand in line. She was amazed Winnie's had gotten so popular.

"Mabel," called Sam. "Come up here and stand with me. Let's have lunch together."

Sam was at the front of the line.

Mabel said, "I don't know if that would be fair, Sam."

People in front of her turned to look at her. She knew they saw an old woman, shrunken and harmless. They motioned her forward. She shrugged and went to stand with him.

"When did Winnie's get so busy?" she asked.

"Well, there's the new website Haley made," he said. "But I think a lot of it's word of mouth. The food's so good no one can stay away."

"I do think you're right," she said, patting his arm. She liked Sam. Had liked him from the moment he'd shown up in town. "When're you going to settle down and get married?" She could say such preposterous things to him without Sam taking offense.

He laughed. "When I meet someone who'll have me. And all my horses."

"That shouldn't be too hard," said Mabel.

"Harder than you think. I don't meet many women."

"But you come here everyday, don't you meet any young women here?"

"No. Not single ones at least."

"Well, I'll keep an eye out for you."

"I'd appreciate it Mabel. You know everybody." He smiled at her. He was such a flirt.

"I do not. So many new people have moved here. And I don't know any of the kids anymore. Not since I stopped teaching."

"Well, you know a lot more people than I do."

Ashley, one of the waitresses, showed them to a table.

"You're busy today," said Sam.

"It's been like this all week. Crazy. Are you here for lunch or dessert?"

"Lunch," said Sam. He looked at Mabel to confirm.

She nodded.

"Well, we're out of bacon, so nothing with bacon on it. And Winnie's still baking so, when dessert rolls around, we'll see what's come out of the oven."

"Yum," said Sam. "I can hardly wait."

They both picked up the menus, but Mabel was staring at the specials' chalkboard on the wall. She put the menu back down.

There was no need to consider the menu. Eddy had made turkey potato chowder. Her mouth watered just reading the specials. She was hungry today. She'd have half a sandwich too. Egg salad sounded good.

She sipped water and debated about coffee, then decided against it. She'd have iced tea today.

Sam put down the menu and said, "You know Bea's granddaughter is in the hospital in Helena?"

"No. I called Bea this morning, but there was no answer. What's wrong?"

"She was playing down by the river and fell, got wedged in between some rocks. Hit her head. She's okay, except for a broken leg."

"Oh, poor thing. Well, I guess that'll slow her down a little."

"But the good thing is, Bea says, Trixie's talking again."

"That's wonderful. Bea told me it's been years since she spoke. Hopefully, it means she's on the mend. I should send her something. What do girls her age like?"

"Trixie? Animals. I'd say animals. But she's got Trouble and Twinkletoes and baby chicks and horses."

"Hmmm. I'll have to think about it. I'd like to send something. Maybe a book."

"While you're sending things, can you send some cooler temperatures, slow the snow melt down?" he asked.

"The river's going to flood this year, isn't it?"

"It already has. Several folks out our way are already getting flooded out. Bea's losing a lot of pasture. And it won't come back when the river goes back down."

"Oh, that's awful."

"She says she's about to give up on cattle."

"That's not where she gets most of her income, is it?"

"I think it's a substantial portion, but I don't really know. She does have a lot of guests at her B and B. And if Haley's websites work the way I think they will, Bea will be flooded with guests."

"Oh, poor Bea. I'll have to call her when she gets back in town. A lot of people are going to have problems with the river. Or maybe they're already having them."

"Around here, I think they already are. People downstream, it'll take a little longer for the flooding to hit there."

"The Blackfoot is unpredictable."

"Yes, she is, but I wouldn't live anywhere else."

"I don't get down to the river very often. I'll hope for some cooler temperatures. So how's your website working?" asked Mabel.

"Great. It's only been up a day and I've already gotten five inquiries about horses for sale. A woman is coming out this afternoon to meet one of the yearlings. That's more action than I had all of last year. Haley's got some kind of magic, that's for sure."

Their lunch arrived and Mabel began to eat.

Her mind wandered off, trying to think about what would help Bea, Haley and Trixie the most. She'd need to make a trip out to Bea's, once they were all back from the hospital.

How could she make an anonymous donation to them?

CHAPTER 21 ~ HALEY

HALEY SPENT THE SECOND NIGHT STRETCHED OVER AN upholstered vinyl chair in Trixie's room. She gave Mom the rollaway cot to sleep on. A nurse had brought it in the first night, apologizing that one was all she could find.

She stood yawning as the nurse came in at six in the morning to take Trixie's vitals. Someone had come in at least twice during the night that Haley had counted. She might have slept through another time. How did they expect people in hospitals to get well if they didn't even get to sleep through the night?

Her neck and back ached. Mom was still sleeping on the cot and Trixie was sound asleep.

Haley rubbed her eyes and walked down to the cafe area and got two cups of coffee and two cream cheese Danish. Then she took the elevator back up to Trixie's room.

By then, Mom was sitting up on the cot, looking bleary eyed, her short gray hair standing up in an odd hairstyle. Trixie was still asleep.

Haley handed Mom a coffee and one of the Danish.

"Thank you."

"You're welcome," said Haley, sitting back in the chair. The Danish was passible as was the coffee. But it was warm and had caffeine in it. She was going to need that today.

Haley must have fallen back asleep. When she woke again, it was nine and Sam was there, talking to Mom and Trixie.

Haley watched them for a few minutes, staring with wonder at her daughter. Who was talking as if it was completely normal for her. As if there hadn't been years of silence.

Trixie asked Sam how the foals were.

"I didn't go over there this morning, but yesterday they were pretty feisty. I can't work one with the other one around. It's too distracting. So you're going to have to get better pretty fast. We've got a lot of work to do with those two little hoodlums."

He glanced at Haley and smiled.

"Well good morning," he said.

"Good morning," she said, trying not to think about how her hair looked. Or her face, or clothes. Then it occurred to her that it had been a long time since she'd worried about that for anyone.

"Sam brought breakfast." said Mom. "Coffee, and quiche from Winnie's."

Haley walked over to the table near Trixie's bed. Sam was unpacking a bag of food. She took one of the paper boxes and a napkin.

Sam poured coffee from a thermos into paper cups he pulled from the bag. He handed Haley a cup.

She took it and sipped the hot liquid. It woke up her mouth and the rich bitter taste flooded her.

"This is awesome coffee, but it's not Winnie's, is it?"

"No. It's mine. I brought that from home. I can make coffee. Quiche, probably not," said Sam.

"Thanks for coming to visit. And for bringing food."

"I figured you might need some real food. Do you know when you're going home?" he asked.

"The doctor hasn't been in yet, has she?" asked Haley.

Sam said, "No. Not yet. The nurse said another couple hours. She said Trixie's doing well this morning."

"Guess we'll find out later when we're going home," said Haley.

Trixie had had to stay in bed all day yesterday. Haley hadn't done much other than walk to the cafe for food or wander the gift shop to buy magazines for all of them to look at.

She set her cup on the window ledge and opened the white cardboard box containing the slice of quiche. The scent of cheddar, basil and tomatoes wafted out, making her stomach growl. She took a plastic fork and dove in. It tasted as extraordinary as it smelled. Winnie made the best quiche.

There was silence in the room as Haley and Mom ate their quiche, Sam sipped his coffee and Trixie ate her oatmeal. No quiche for her. She had to have hospital food.

After Trixie's breakfast, a nurse or therapist, came in with a pair of crutches for Trixie and showed her how to use them. Then the woman took her for a walk around the floor. By the time she got back to the room, Trixie's face was red from exertion.

"You'll need to work on that upper body strength," said Haley.

Trixie nodded, sinking back onto her bed, looking relieved.

Finally, Dr. Tanner came in. She sent everyone out of the room and examined Trixie. They lingered in the hall outside of the room.

She came out and said to Haley, "Your daughter's doing quite well. I've sent a message to Dr. Jackson in Lincoln, who I'm referring her to. I want him to see her tomorrow and make sure everything's still okay. But my feeling is that after lunch, she can go home. Just make her take it easy for a couple of days. It'll take a while for her to get used to the crutches and I don't want her whacking her head again."

Haley nodded and got all the information about Dr. Jackson's number and address as well as pain medication for Trixie. Just in case she needed it.

She saw an elderly woman who looked vaguely familiar get off the elevator. The woman wore a lilac colored light coat and walked up to Bea, who looked surprised and hugged her.

It wasn't until then that Haley could place the woman. She was Mabel. Mrs. McTavish, her old teacher.

Haley finished talking with Dr. Tanner who went off to see another patient.

"I drove over with Sam. We ate lunch together at Winnie's yesterday and he suggested it. Said, you'd all be going stir crazy. And I had baby blankets to deliver here to the hospital, so here I am," Mabel said.

"Well, it's great to see you Mabel," said Mom.

"We can go back in now," said Haley.

They opened the door and Trixie said, "I get to go home today, don't I?"

"Yep," said Haley.

"Yay. I miss Twink and Trouble so much!"

Mabel had been carrying a purple plastic bag and she handed it to Trixie.

"I wanted to get you a little something, Sam said you like animals, but that you had plenty around. So, this is just a substitute, for when you can't be around them."

Trixie pulled a black and white stuffed cat out of the bag.

"Oh, this is so soft," she said, hugging the cat. "Thank you so much, Mabel. I really appreciate it."

"You're very welcome. None of us are too old for stuffed animals," Mabel said, winking.

Haley would have thought Trixie was too old, but she noticed her daughter didn't stop hugging the cat until her lunch came. Then she tucked the cat beneath her blankets, so she wouldn't spill food on it. As soon as lunch was over and the tray moved, Trixie took the cat back out and hugged it again.

For the trip home, they decided to switch cars. Mabel would ride home with Mom. Sam had a large pickup with a crew cab. There was enough leg room for Trixie to ride in the back seat with her leg straight out. Haley rode in front.

Sam talked to her about how much he liked the new website. His email was full of enquiries about the horses. His voicemail was packed with more serious enquiries. And a woman had come out yesterday and bought a mare, promising to come back for another next month when she had more money. It looked like his business was finally going to get off the ground.

Haley smiled. Her website mojo was working.

Mabel was enjoying riding back to Lincoln with Bea. It wasn't often that she got to be someone else's passenger. Bea was driving her Nissan SUV. It was a brilliant blue color. It was newer than any of her vehicles and Mabel leaned back in the cushy seat and relaxed, looking at the scenery.

They were driving past grasslands. A rainbow of grasses passed by: dusky rose, wheat yellow, and sage green. The land was fenced with wire and wood posts. Near one section a small herd of pronghorn antelope were jumping a fence. Their white bellies and rumps made them stand out, There were about seven of them. The car moved too fast for her to count.

"Pronghorn," she pointed.

"Oh my, aren't they beautiful."

She held her breath watching them. They weren't that common of a sight, lovely graceful creatures. A nice part of the wild in a mostly tamed area.

Bea was quiet, but happy. Mabel knew she was tired, but so relieved Trixie was going to be all right and that she was speaking again.

Mabel sipped a coke she'd gotten just before they left town.

It was bitter, watered down. She remembered when coke used to be quite sweet, not this awful stuff. Bea had been wise to get coffee. It was probably better. At least it smelled good in the car.

She'd had a pleasant ride over with Sam, who it turned out had a thing for Haley. Although Mabel didn't think he'd told anyone about it. He just glowed when he talked about her. Mabel wasn't sure whether to tell Bea. Probably best to let it come out in its own time.

It was times like this Mabel regretted that she and Mac hadn't had children. They'd never wanted any when they were younger. Now that she was older, Mabel had to admit it felt sad to be alone so much. It was probably time to go get an apartment in one of those retirement communities where they had a lot of social activities. She wasn't sure she'd fit in though and didn't want to leave Lincoln.

"How's your B and B business going?" asked Mabel.

"You know, I hate to admit it, but the website hasn't been up long and I'm getting a lot more reservations. I didn't think this new website thing would work. I think we're going to be able to get a hot tub this summer. Like Haley wanted. That'll make guests happy."

"I'm so glad. Winnie's place has been hopping every time I go by. I'm going to have to make reservations soon. And it's not even summer yet."

"Well, I guess this website business is here to stay."

"It's amazing. I don't have a computer at home, but I use one at the library and I'm amazed at what you can find out about the world."

"I don't use mine for anything except business,' said Bea.

"You should give it a try sometime. I could have used one when I was a teacher, I'll tell you that. It would have saved me so much time."

"Times have sure changed," said Bea. "How are you getting on these days?"

"Oh, I'm doing fine, but I'm getting tired of living alone, I think. I might have to move to Helena or Missoula to get into one of those retirement homes."

"Your health is good isn't it?"

"Just fine. I'm not talking about a nursing home. A retirement home is just an apartment for old people, except they cook for you. Not as good as Winnie and Eddy though. The retirement homes have social dos and crafts and such. Even field trips. Problem is, I don't want to have to move to another town. Start all over again. I don't want to leave my friends."

"Why don't you move in with us?" asked Bea.

Mabel stared at her.

"We've got space," said Bea.

"But you'd lose a room for your B and B."

"I'm planning on building an addition. And you'd have guests to hang out with, they almost always want to know the history of this area. And you'd have Haley, Trixie, Jerry and Dani and maybe even me for company. I'm going to hire someone else to help clean in a couple weeks. You'd be more than welcome."

"It sounds like you've got quite a houseful."

"I do, but I'd love to have you there. Keep you out of trouble." Bea smiled at her.

Mabel wondered for a fleeting second if Bea knew about the robberies. No, that was just crazy.

"Well, I'd have to pay you. I wouldn't feel good about it other wise. Because with you doing all that cooking and buying food, ..."

"We can agree on something, I'm sure. I can clear one of the rooms out completely if you want to bring your own furniture.

Can't give you a separate living room, bathroom and kitchen like those fancy retirement homes though."

Mabel laughed. "Well, I'll think about it. It might just be what I'm looking for."

"It'd be fun having you out at the ranch. Give me someone my age to talk to."

"I'd have to sell Mac's old cars first. And get rid of a lot of stuff, that should have been gone twenty years ago."

"Just let me know when you're ready, so I can save you a room."

"I'll do that."

Mabel sipped on her soda and watched the mountains fly by. The highway had climbed up higher now, cutting through the passes.

The sky began to darken with small shapes.

"Oh my gosh. Look," said Bea, pointing. She pulled to the side of the road at a pullout and got out, walking around to Mabel's side. Mabel got out of the car too. The cool air felt bracing.

In the sky, the shapes grew larger and larger as they came closer. They flew towards the north.

"They're golden eagles, I'll bet," said Bea. "I've always heard they migrate at this time of year. Over Roger's Pass. I've never seen it. Not once in my whole life. Not till now."

Mabel could hear the occasional screeching of an eagle. They were huge. She knew they were even larger than bald eagles, which she'd seen once. Up here in the mountains, close to the sky and those rain clouds and the eagles passing, she felt part of nature. Part of the world again.

CHAPTER 23 ~ HALEY

Haley felt relieved to be back at Mom's. She sat outside at the wood picnic table on the patio. Above her stretched the solid roof that connected to the house, keeping off the rain. Haley sipped mint iced tea and watching Trixie feed the chickens in the rain. They really were chickens already. Their fluffy down was giving way to actual feathers. They looked as awkward as Trixie did, hobbling around on her crutches. But she'd insisted.

The trip home from the hospital had been uncomfortable. Haley had the feeling Sam was trying to say something to her. He'd start talking, then realize Trixie was there and stop. As if what he wanted to say wasn't for her ears.

The conversation they did have felt stilted. And after two nights of sleeping upright in the chair, she'd felt too exhausted to try and make small talk.

That was two days ago. He hadn't been over to work with the foals since.

She should probably drop by his house. See what he wanted. Today, before she lost her nerve.

Mom came out of the house with a glass of iced tea, wiping

sweat from her forehead. She'd been baking cornbread to go with the chili for dinner. And boysenberry pies.

"I'm going to run over to Sam's for a few minutes," said Haley.

"Okay," said Mom, looking at her strangely.

Haley rarely went anywhere.

"Can you keep an eye on Trixie for me?"

"I think she's doing fine," said Mom. "But I'll keep tabs on her."

"Okay."

Haley decided to drive. It would be faster. There was still a lot to do today. More guests coming in tonight.

She ran for her car, trying to not get too drenched, and drove the two minutes to his house. He came out of the house as she drove up.

He wore a rain-spattered green t-shirt, jeans and boots. He really was a handsome guy. Suddenly, she felt stupid. But Haley decided to just deal with it the way she always did, pretend to felt confident.

"Hello," he said, as she got out of her car.

"Hi," she said, shading her eyes from the rain. The rain wasn't going to help the flooding situation at all. It had been pouring for the last twenty-four hours, at least.

"What brings you to this neck of the woods?" he motioned her towards the big covered porch in front of his house.

She followed, trying to find the right words. How to say it?

"I had the feeling you wanted to talk to me the other day, but Trixie was there. And I was a basket case. Too sleep deprived."

"I did. And you're right. I didn't want to sat anything in front of Trixie. She's just started talking. I didn't want to screw that up. There were a couple things. First, I wanted to let you know that Frank's been a great help with his wolf. And a lot of the other folks around town have been being unfriendly to your ex. He's not gone yet, but we're making progress."

"Thank you," she said. "I feel like I should be fighting my own battles. But I've never made any progress with him."

"Sometimes it takes a village," he said, wiping the rain off his face.

"And the second thing?" she asked, leaning against her car.

He looked down at his feet, then said, "Oh yeah, I wanted to tell you that the website looks amazing. Absolutely stunning. I've gotten so many calls and emails about horses for sale. I've got people coming every day this week to look at a horse. So, thank you."

"You're welcome. I really enjoyed doing it."

He'd already told her that. On the drive back from Helena.

"Well, it's great. I've been raving about it to everyone I know," he said.

She nodded. Why couldn't he have said this in front of Trixie?

There was an awkward silence. Haley thought maybe she should go.

"The other thing was, I don't know how to do this anymore. Maybe I never did. I don't want to make you feel uncomfortable, but I'm interested in you. No. That's not the right word. I never have the right words around you. I'm fascinated by you. Attracted to you. I want to take you out, but I have no idea if you're even open to such a thing."

Ah, there it was. That's what was going on underneath the surface. She hadn't seen that at all. She thought the attraction was all from her side.

"I'm interested," she said. "I have been ever since I met you. Life has just been sort of crazy."

He nodded.

"How about dinner tomorrow night?"

"I think I could swing that," she said. "But I have to be home early. I need to get up early. I'm the laundry slave."

He laughed.

"So, where are we going? How should I dress? Casual, formal? I haven't been on a date in so many years, I have no idea."

"Casual or dressy, whatever you're in the mood for. I'll find a place over in Missoula, away from prying eyes. Pick you up at five?"

"Okay," she said. "Well, I'd better get back. I've got a lot of work to get done."

"More websites?"

"Well, those too. But first, there's laundry. You would not believe how much laundry a B and B goes through: sheets, bath towels, kitchen towels, rags, potholders. Not to mention clothes for Mom, Trixie and I."

"Bea needs to hire a full time laundry person."

"She has. I'm it. Can't complain though, cause the bed's comfy and the food is good."

Haley got in the car and waved as she drove off, feeling jittery and on edge. She had a date. Haley hadn't had a date in over fourteen years. However was she going to survive?

CHAPTER 24 ~ MABEL

Mabel stood in the immaculate garage, staring at all the cars and pickups. She felt exhausted, but it was done. Each one was spotless. It had taken her seven days. One day per vehicle. And for good measure she'd also cleaned the green Subaru, which she was keeping.

Each one had been vacuumed and scrubbed down on the inside and out. Even underneath. Just as Mac had showed her all those years ago. There was not a speck of dust to be sneezed at in the entire garage.

She'd also rummaged through her paperwork and found the titles for each one. Gary was coming tomorrow to look at them. Gary's brother sold used cars in Great Falls and hired Gary to search for cars to buy and make sure each one was running well. Mabel had always called him when she'd had a problem or needed maintenance done.

Once all the vehicles were gone, she'd work on paring down belongings in the house. Then she'd talk to a real estate agent about selling her house. Find out what needed to be done to spruce it up.

She stood with her hands on her hips smiling. Yes, things were working out nicely.

Inside the house, the phone rang. She thought about ignoring it, but ran for it anyway. She got there just in time. It was Winnie.

"Mabel, I don't know if you've heard, but they're evacuating everyone down by the river."

"What?"

"They're evacuating all the folks down by the river. Expecting major flooding within the next 24 hours. I thought you'd want to know."

"So, Bea and her family?"

"Yes."

"Do they need a place to stay?"

Winnie said, "I don't know. I expect Bea's trying to move livestock at the moment. Sam too. I know they're opening up the high school gym for people to sleep in."

"Okay, I'll make up my two spare bedrooms. Just in case and go down to the gym. See what I can do to help. Thank you for letting me know."

"You're welcome. I've gotta get back to work. People will be needing food without their kitchens. We're opening for dinner until this is all over."

Mabel hung up. She couldn't remember people out by Bea's ever having to evacuate. The flooding must be really bad this year. She hoped people wouldn't lose their homes.

Pouring a glass of orange juice, she drank the tangy liquid. The cold felt good in her mouth. She was hot today, with all that cleaning. Held the cool glass up to her cheeks to cool them. It felt good on her warm skin.

After she finished drinking, Mabel washed the glass with a soapy sponge, rinsed it in cool water and set it in the dish drainer to dry.

Then she scurried around, putting fresh sheets on the beds

in both spare bedrooms. She'd taken all the blankets and bedspreads off, stuffing them in the dryer to freshen up and get the dust off. Then quickly vacuumed her house and finished remaking the beds.

As an afterthought, she cut some of the daffodils out front and put them in three vases. One in each guest room and the last on the kitchen table. That ought to add some cheer to an awful situation. She called Bea and left a message on her answering machine to come on over to the school and meet her to pick up the key to the house.

Mabel changed into clean clothes. Burgundy pants and a rose pink blouse. Then she put her walking shoes back on and grabbed her maroon sweater. She left her purse at home and slipped the keys, and the extra house key, into her pants pocket after locking up.

It was a beautifully warm day. That must be why it was flooding. The end of April and it was in the mid-60's. The weatherman said the temperature was running five to ten degrees above average. This was the end of May temperatures. The snow was melting way too fast.

She walked briskly to the high school. She'd sure been getting a lot of exercise lately and it didn't seem likely to end soon. Well, it kept her busy.

Inside the big gym, volunteers were beginning to gather. Many had brought bedding, sleeping bags and mats.

Fred Katzen was organizing things. That was good, he'd make sure nothing slipped through the cracks. She waited until it was her turn.

"What can I do Fred?" she asked.

"Mabel. Well, I don't rightly know yet. People haven't begun to arrive. I think they're still battening down the hatches at their houses."

"Well, surely I can do something." She knew he was thinking she was too old to be of any good.

"You used to teach. There'll be lots of kids here with stressed out parents. Can you gather up some materials from the teachers maybe, something that will keep the kids entertained? Maybe sign up some of the teachers to help you, I don't know. Have crafts or something for them to do."

"I can do that," she said.

It was Tuesday. Classes were in session. She glanced at the clock. Ten. She might be able to catch teachers on their morning breaks.

"How many are we expecting?"

"At least seventy adults, maybe thirty kids. Maybe more."

"Okay, I'll get started. Where can I set up?" she asked.

"They're setting up tables for kids' lunch in the far corner. Maybe you can wangle one away from them and put it over there," he said, pointing.

"Okay."

Mabel went over to two young men, who she didn't recognize. They were setting up rows of tables. The gym doubled as a cafeteria, so there were enough tables to fill the entire space if need be.

"Gentlemen, can I bother you for a minute?" she asked, sweetly.

"Certainly Ma'am," said the man with a beard.

"Please call me Mabel. I need two tables set up in that far corner. Is it possible you could do that for me?"

"Certainly Mabel," said the taller one. "What are they for?"

"Oh, I get to entertain the kids when they show up."

"What are you going to do with them?" asked the bearded man.

"I think we'll start with watercolors. Most kids love painting. It's messy and even the older ones can get into it."

"You're a brave woman, Mabel," said the tall one.

"You don't live this long without being brave," she said, winking at them.

It took her an hour to gather up supplies from both the elementary and the high school: paper, paint, brushes, paper towels and plastic water glasses. Eventually, she had it all. One of the teachers sent a couple of students along to carry the supplies. Another teacher donated play dough for really young children. Four teachers said they'd be over to help as soon as school ended.

She knew everyone looked at her and saw a small, helpless old woman. Sometimes being old was an advantage. At least she knew how to take advantage of it.

When she returned to the gym, accompanied by the two students and the supplies, people were beginning to trickle in. Adults only so far. Most of their kids were still in school.

Mabel pinned up three posters to the bulletin board in that corner of the gym. Then she took markers and made a quick sign on poster board. It read *Entertainment Corner*. She tucked the art supplies in a nearby closet.

One of the teachers who was coming after school had volunteered to bring over some games. So Mabel got the gentlemen to set up another table for that. She had seats for thirty. That should be enough. Some kids wouldn't want to join in. They'd want to be on their phones.

Mabel took a break and went to Winnie's for lunch. The cafe was nearly empty of locals, but there were a few tourists. Most people were probably off helping their neighbors move.

She waved at Winnie who was busy in the kitchen. Mabel ate a juicy burger and drank some coffee. She had a feeling it would be a long day.

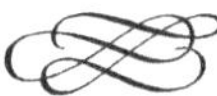

Haley sat on Sooty in the hot sun, her hands in leather gloves resting on the saddle horn. Waiting for the sheriff to temporarily close the nearly empty highway. Two cars passed and he did.

She clucked the buckskin gelding into motion, followed by a train of six other horses. They'd all been saddled, so a separate load of tack wouldn't have to be driven over. The horses were all feeling skittish and jumpy. They'd caught the humans' anxiety.

She smelled the sweat from her horse. Not that he was working hard, he was just stressed out too. The horses knew the water was rising. They'd seen it from their pasture. Taking down Ponderosa pines which stood a couple hundred feet tall and hundreds of years old. The sound of the river alone was unnerving. A roaring monster eating everything in its path.

Small wonder the horses were nervous. When she'd gone out this morning they were all crowded at the section of the pasture farthest from the river, wild eyed.

Mom followed behind, leading six other horses. The most skittish horses, along with the two foals and their moms, had already been trailered over to the Jensen's property earlier in the morning.

Behind Mom, Jerry, Dani, Sam, Don Jensen and Trouble, were herding the cattle. Trouble was a good herding dog, obeying the signals given him. After they finished with the cattle, they'd go back to Sam's and lead the rest of his horses over to the Jensens. He'd also trailered the younger ones, their dams and his stallion, over earlier in the morning.

Jensen's ranch and all their pastures lay on the other side of the highway, about five miles down the road. They were on much higher ground and wouldn't get flooded.

The Blackfoot was rising quickly, swallowing Mom's pastureland and heading towards the barn. The barn wouldn't win if the river rose much higher. Those buildings couldn't withstand the force of the water. If the river swelled even more, which was expected over the coming days, the house might flood too. Haley didn't want to think about that.

Last night her date with Sam never happened. Instead, they'd been told by Sheriff Allen that they'd have to evacuate today. So, they'd begun the long process of planning what to do.

They'd gotten all the tack out. Dani and Jerry had packed up their staff cabins. Mom had filled her car with the important stuff, including the new computer, all her business records and old photographs. She'd taken the chickens and Twinkletoes over to the Jensens last night.

Trixie was back at the house, packing up her few things, moving slowly because of the crutches. Haley had already gotten her own things in the car. She was grateful they didn't have more than would fit in her Toyota.

Her mouth felt dry as she rode along the highway. Why hadn't she brought a water bottle? Haley tried to breathe deeply and relax, hoping that would spread to the horses, give them the chance to relax. She wiped the sweat off her forehead with the gloves. Shifted in the saddle.

The horses' hooves click-clacked on the asphalt, followed by the mooing cows. She could hear Jerry and Dani whistling and directing Trouble, keeping the cattle in a tight bunch. It wouldn't be good if they wandered off into the woods.

One of the mares she was leading, Sadie, started to trot faster, threatening to take the lead. Haley turned Sooty in a circle away from her, forcing Sadie to do a little extra work and move on the outside of the circle.

"Sadie, behave yourself," said Haley. The horse didn't understand her words, but she'd catch the intent. Just like having a teenager.

After a couple of circles, Sadie settled back down and they continued onward.

Haley decided she probably should have ridden Sadie. Troublesome horse. Might be the next horse to get sold. Sadie was only rarely given to guests to ride. She needed a strong rider.

It was taking longer than it should have to make it to the Jensens. Haley had to circle twice more and finally had to stop. Dani rode forward and clipped the horse she'd been riding to the lead. He was better behaved. Then Dani smoothly slid over onto Sadie, unclipped her and took the troublesome mare off to herd cattle.

They finally rode up the Jensen's gravel driveway. About half a mile up from the highway the driveway opened out into pastures and the ranch house sat perched on a short bluff overlooking the highway. With the rise in elevation, Haley could see above the tree line to mountains in the distance.

They put all of Mom's horses in an empty pasture along with the cattle. There was enough grass for a few days. They tied all the horses up to the rail fence, unbridled and unsaddled them, then turned them loose. All except for the ones they were riding back to Sam's.

Trouble was taken to the kitchen so he could eat dinner.

They'd keep him inside along with Twink, who was already there. Both of them were likely to be confused with the new surroundings.

As they left, she could hear Sam's stallion calling to the newly arrived mares. He ran up and down the fence line of the pasture he was in, prancing, tossing his long mane and then bucking. Showing off.

The trip back to Sam's was faster. They haltered up his remaining horses, saddling up only three. Sam didn't have many saddles. He didn't lead trail rides like Mom did.

Mom walked back to her house to get her car and check on Trixie.

Sam, Dani, Jerry and Haley took off down the highway with Sam's horses. His horses were mostly young and skittish, but each person was only leading two. Most of them had rarely been led by being clipped to another horse, so the trip was a challenge. There was a lot of stopping, but eventually they made it to Jensens' and got Sam's horses into the pasture with his stallion and the other mares.

They put Mom's horses in with her other horses and the cattle. There wasn't room for Mom, Trixie or Haley. They'd find somewhere else to stay. Jerry and Dani would be coming back here to help the Jensen's watch the horses and cattle. And Sam would be staying at the Jensen's too.

Haley called Mom on the phone and said, "We're done here."

"Okay," said Mom. "Just in time. Trixie and I just watched the barn go."

"Crap. I was hoping it wouldn't."

"Me too," Mom said, sadly. "Well, I'll come get you all, so all of you can get your cars and clear out."

In five minutes they were driving back to Sam's. They dropped him off to get his truck and then went to Mom's, where Dani and Jerry each got their cars. They were staying in the Jensen's bunkhouses.

Mom had been talking to the sheriff. He was directing everyone who was evacuating to go into town to the high school. Haley quickly hauled the rest of Trixie's belongings out to the car. Trixie got in, looking relieved.

"Watching the barn being ripped down was scary," she said.

"I know honey. I'll be back in a minute. Just gonna check on Mom."

"Okay." Trixie pulled out her phone and began playing a game. Her hands shaking slightly.

Haley went back in the house. Mom was staring out the open back door. She wasn't crying, but her lower lip was quivering. Haley hugged her.

"I'm going to miss this place," Mom said.

"You never know. It might be here when you get back."

Mom looked at her.

"Okay, it probably won't. But you've got good insurance. You'll rebuild. People have lived in this area for a hundred fifty years. The water's never gotten this high before. It probably won't get this high again in our lifetime. You got the important stuff out."

"I know. It's just sentiment. The tools, the chicken coop that I built. My garden. The furniture."

"Well, say goodbye and let's get going, before we're lost too."

The raging river had taken the entire pasture that the horses had just left and now had risen to just the other side of the gravel service road. It wouldn't take much for it to get to the house and the other cabins behind the garden. They would be rebuilding. Provided there was any land left to rebuild on.

Mom closed the door, locked it and said, "Let's go." She had picked up an old empty vase, made of pale orange carnival glass, as she went.

Haley got in her car and waited to leave, watching her mom lock the front door, wipe at her face and get in her car. Then they drove off to town. It was nearly two. They'd missed lunch.

She sighed, feeling the loss of most of the ranch.

Would the house be there when they got back?

CHAPTER 26 ~ MABEL

Mabel was walking around the table, helping the younger children with their paints. School was out. The gym was getting very crowded as people swarmed in. They needed to turn the ventilation system up higher. The big building stank of too many people. Too many people who smelled like wet dogs. And it felt cramped.

She said to one little girl, "Here dear, you want to wash your brush out really well between colors, unless you want everything to be brown. Are you trying to make this yellow?"

The girl with big brown eyes nodded.

"Okay then. We'll just use this paper towel to blot up the paint. See? Now, your brush is all clean and you can dip it into the yellow and it will work now."

The girl did and smiled as the sun she was painting a picture of turned yellow.

"Perfect," said Mabel. She moved on around the table.

Another group came in the door. She saw Bea, Haley and Trixie, moving slowly on her crutches.

Mabel said to one of the teachers who was helping her, "I'm going to take a break."

"Go ahead. Thanks for setting all this up."

"It's been a pleasure. Sometimes I really miss teaching."

Mabel walked over to the sign in desk and said to Bea, "Good afternoon. I've got room at my house for all of you, if you want to sleep on beds."

"Oh my goodness Mabel. Thank you. We'd love to," said Bea.

Haley and Trixie nodded.

"I don't think I'd be able to stand up again once I got down on the floor," said Trixie, looking down at her crutches.

"You and me both," said Bea.

"Well, I walked over, but if you want to give me a ride, we can go get you settled in."

Mabel rode back home in Bea's car, holding a vase Bea had stuffed into the front seat, along with her computer. She chewed some spearmint gum one of the volunteers had been passing around. It had lost all its flavor, but she hadn't had time to throw it away.

"I don't know why I saved that old thing," said Bea, gesturing to the vase. "I guess I just wanted to save one more thing as I left, anything from the damn river."

"It must be hard walking away from your home, knowing it might not be there when you get back."

"I hate feeling helpless."

Mabel nodded.

When they got to her house Mabel said, "Why don't I pull a couple of the cars out of my garage. Let you gals park there. You've got so much stuff in your cars. I wouldn't want anything to get stolen."

She got out, opened the garage doors and pulled her green Subaru out and then the dark blue Suburban, parking them in front of the closed garage doors that sat behind other cars.

Once Haley and Bea had parked inside, Mabel closed the

garage doors and locked them. They followed her into the house through the adjoining door.

The day had gotten into the seventies. She could see that Haley's shirt was damp from all the work of moving horses and packing cars. The scent of the freshly cut daffodils filled the kitchen.

Haley carried her flowered bag that was just like Trixie's.

"Bea, here's your room, Haley here's your room and Trixie, here's yours. The bathroom's right there and I'll be in the kitchen. I know I've got some extra keys. Do you gals need some lunch?"

"No," said Bea. "We just came from Winnie's."

"Okay."

Mabel went into the kitchen and opened her odds and ends drawer. There was a small bowl in it containing keys. She wasn't sure what they all belonged to though. Finally, after trying several, she found two more house and garage keys. She put them on two empty keychains and laid them on the kitchen table. It would be fun having guests. She only wished the circumstances weren't so awful.

She mixed up some iced tea and put it in the fridge to chill. There was already lemonade in there.

Bea came in and sat down at the table.

"What should we make for dinner?" she asked.

"Well, I don't know what you folks like," said Mabel.

"At my house, people eat what's on the table or they fend for themselves. Of course, the paying guests have different rules."

"I've got some steak in the refrigerator. And corn on the cob."

"That sounds lovely. Do you have a barbecue?"

"Out in the back yard. It hasn't seen much use lately. But I do have briquets. Oh and I've got ice cream for dessert."

"I think that's perfect. I'm happy to make it all if you want," said Bea.

"Well, I probably should get back to the high school. The painting was my idea."

"I'm pooped after moving all those critters, otherwise I'd come help," said Bea.

"Well, of course you are. You all stay here. I'll be back around 5:00 p.m., after I've helped clean up the painting mess."

"Thank you so much Mabel," said Haley.

"So, here are the keys, one for the house, and this one's for the garage. Just make sure you lock up if you leave. And I've got my cell phone if you have any other questions."

"We'll be fine," said Bea.

"Okay, there's lemonade and ice tea in the refrigerator and ice cubes in the freezer," she said, sliding her cell phone and keys into her pant's pockets.

"Thanks," said Bea.

She went out the front door and with a quick clip walked towards the highway and towards the high school. As Mabel passed the grocery store, she noticed the lot was full. People stocking up.

The parking lot at Fischer's Motel was full and the neon sign out front flashed *NO VACANCY*.

She saw that man's car, Haley's ex, was parked there again. That wasn't good news. Frank Helmsman's wolf hadn't worked to scare him away. She'd have to warn them when she got back home. They'd be safe till then, unpacking and tired. It was a good thing Mabel had seen them at the school and got them to her house.

When she got to the high school, even more people had arrived. Where had they all come from? She hadn't known that many people lived around here.

Pretty soon they'd have to open up the elementary school and middle school gym.

Mabel helped clean up the painting aftermath. The kids had

moved on to board games. She and the remaining teacher stowed the paint in the supply cupboard.

As she wiped down the table with a couple of wet paper towels, Mabel saw Haley's ex walk in the door.

His weaselly eyes looked around.

For Haley and Trixie.

She was glad they were at her house. This one wasn't giving up easily.

CHAPTER 27 ~ HALEY

Haley sat at Mabel's kitchen table. She sipped her glass of lemonade. It tasted awful. Too sweet and full of nasty chemicals. Clearly from a mix.

That was ungrateful. Mabel was giving them a place to stay. And she was in her 70's. Haley would be lucky to still be mobile at that age.

She felt tired. That was all.

She'd just loaded everything the two of them owned into the car. Once again. Then unloaded part of it. Then half of Mom's stuff. And helped Mom cancel reservations because of the flooding.

It felt as if she'd spent the last nine years packing and unpacking. She and Trixie had moved several times during each of those years. Each move paring away more of their belongings until this last time, for the move back to Lincoln, everything they owned had fit into the Toyota.

She was tired of it. She wanted a home. Had thought they'd found one. Now it looked like Mom was going to be homeless too. They wouldn't know what happened until the river went down and they could go back and have a look.

That would be a while. The water was still rising and the snow still melting. Fast. The temperatures were going up, not down. The Blackfoot was slated to crest in a couple of days.

Mom came into the room and plopped down in a chair at the table.

"I'm pooped," said Haley

"Me too," said Mom

"I can grill the steaks," said Haley. "I'll go light the coals. Get them going. Mabel should be back in a bit. It's after five."

"How's Trixie doing?"

"Fine. She's tired too. She's actually napping," said Haley.

"I don't think she slept well last night. She's gotten used to sleeping with Twink."

"I hadn't thought about that. I know the river's been making her scared."

"It's been scaring everyone. I'm relieved we got all the animals out at least," said Mom.

"Me too. Well, where do you think Mabel keeps her matches?"

Mom held up some matches that sat by a candle on the windowsill.

"I'll go start coals."

She went out the back door. The yard was small. A concrete patio covered with a roof to keep the sun off, surrounded by a patch of straggly grass and weeds. A wooden picnic table with benches sat on the patio, plus an ancient copper colored barbecue. It looked like it had been around for at least fifty years. About a foot and a half wide with a nearly flat bottom and a metal back, that must be a wind shield, covered half the circumference.

Mabel had left a bag of briquets and a can of lighter fluid on the table.

Haley took the grill off and set an old rusty coffee can with holes in it on the bottom rack. She poured the charcoal into the coffee can, sprinkled them with lighter fluid, then lit the coals. Smoke swirled around her.

She didn't have to do laundry at least. The next few days she'd be able to work on the new websites she'd contracted out for. She could at least write the text. She'd have to drive somewhere and find wifi to upload everything. But those contracts would bring in some more money. Because Mom had to cancel reservations for the next month for the B and B. It would be even longer if the house went.

The river had rarely come up onto the ranch that far. They were in the hundred year flood area. Apparently, this was that hundred years.

When they returned to the ranch, they'd need to concentrate on putting up fencing and buying feed. There probably wouldn't be anything resembling grass left. Maybe not even topsoil. And they couldn't leave the animals at Jensen's for long. Couldn't use up all their pastureland.

There might be some federal disaster money coming in, the Governor had said on tv last night. Because everyone downstream of them was getting hammered too. Lincoln was just the beginning of the flooding because it was up in the mountains near the Continental Divide.

Haley sat on the picnic table, her feet on the bench and looked at the cloudless sky. A flock of hundreds of large birds passed over. Golden eagles. They liked to catch the wind over the pass and float eastward. This was probably the last of the migration. She assumed they knew the climate was warming up and they compensated. Migrating earlier each year.

They were on the move just like her. Except she didn't want to be. She wanted a permanent home.

Her mouth still tasted like the lemonade. Maybe she should go over to the grocery store and pick up a bottle of wine for dinner. Haley got up and went inside.

"Mom, could you keep an eye on the coals for me?"

"Sure," came Mom's voice from the living room. "Why?"

Haley heard the tv news on in the background.

"I thought I'd go to the grocery store and pick up a bottle of wine for dinner. Mabel doesn't have a problem with alcohol does she?"

"No. She drinks occasionally. Good idea."

Haley dumped the rest of her lemonade down the sink and rinsed out the glass. Then she walked down the hall to her bedroom, grabbed her small purse, slipped her phone in it and put the long strap on one shoulder across her body with the bag on her opposite hip.

She went to the front door and said, "Okay, I'll be back in just a few minutes."

The grocery store was only a block away. Mabel lived close to everything.

She passed Winnie's. Winnie was just getting in their car. Eddy was filling up their trunk with large white to-go boxes.

"I'm taking pies over to the gym," she said.

"My goodness, how many did you make?"

"Ten apple and ten huckleberry."

"You've been baking all day haven't you?"

"Since 3 a.m. I started early today. They said there's over 150 people at the gym already. They're expecting a few more will show up as the river rises. We're open for dinner until people can go back home."

"Winnie, take care of yourself. Don't wear yourself out."

"I won't, but I'll tell you, I feel more energized baking all day, than I do baking and then waiting tables."

"Well, then you need to hire more wait staff, don't you?"

"I certainly do. Well, gotta run these over, so they can have them for dessert."

"Okay, we'll see you. We're staying at Mabel's."

"Oh good. I'm glad you pried Bea out of her house. I was worried."

"She's not happy. The barn's gone and the house might be gone by now, too."

"Oh no. That's awful. You gals stop by for lunch tomorrow, okay?"

"I think that would be a good idea," said Haley.

She continued on to the grocery store. It was more crowded than usual. But she'd been there early in the day mostly. This was after work and during a crisis. People were buying a lot of food. Stocking up.

Haley went to the wine area. She finally chose a red blend and walked towards the cash registers. They'd set up an express lane, so she stood in that line, six people in front of her.

She read the magazine covers at the checkout stand. Not recognizing any of the names. That's what came of not watching tv or movies anymore. She was always working.

"Haley," said a male voice.

She looked up to see James, her ex.

"How are you?" he asked, smiling his slimy smile.

She felt paralyzed. Couldn't speak. Her mouth felt dry as sandy prairie. Grit filled her mouth.

Finally, she hissed, "Get out of my life."

"Can't do that, I'm afraid. I'm Trixie's father. You can't keep her away from me."

"You ceased to be her father when you hospitalized me."

"That's not the way my lawyer sees it. She says I can get custody. You can't even hold a job. Not even a job as a waitress. And you fled the state. Trixie's not registered for school."

"She's done for this grade. Out of school till fall."

"You're not a fit mother. We're going to prove it in court. Then Trixie will come live with me. I can give her everything she needs."

"No. They'll never find you a fit parent," she said, knowing they could.

She'd moved up the line to checkout, finally set the bottle of wine down on the counter.

"You'll see," he said, leaving the store.

Haley paid for the wine. As she left the store, she looked around for him, for a car that might be his. She was shaking, but wouldn't let him or anyone see it.

Not wanting to go back to Mabel's in case he was following her, she went over to the mercantile store. Trixie needed some new clothes. Haley had meant to take a trip into Helena and get them. But this was as good a time as any. Half an hour later her phone chirped and she answered.

"Haley, are you coming back? It's been an hour. I grilled the steaks and we're ready to eat."

"I'm sorry Mom. I was at the grocery store and James came in and threatened to take Trixie away from me. I didn't want to go straight back to Mabel's. Didn't want to be followed. So I'm at Johnson's. Thought if I shopped he might go away. I don't want him to find Trixie."

"Did he follow you there?"

"I don't know. I don't know what kind of car he drives these days."

"I'll come pick you up and we can drive around and lose him," said Mom.

"No, you stay and eat. I'll be okay."

She heard Mom talking to Mabel.

"Oh, Mabel says to ask to go out their back door."

"Good idea. I'll be back soon."

Haley paid and was out the back door in minutes. She'd bought a straw cowboy hat and tucked her hair up in it, covered her own green t-shirt with a blue hoody. She kept her head down and ran down the alley and at the next street went another street away from the highway.

After half a block, she turned behind to look. Not a car on the road. She backtracked to Mabel's and hurried inside.

Out of breath, she closed the door behind her. He hadn't followed her. So that was good. It was a small thing though. She was running again. Like a frightened deer before the roaring river. This was no way to live.

Mom came out of the kitchen, a worried look on her face.

"I'm okay. I got away out the back door. He didn't follow me."

She took off the cowboy hat and her now damp hair fell in place. She put her bags down on the hallway table, handing the wine to Mom. Then unzipped the hoody and took it off. She was way too hot.

"Come out to the back. We're eating at the picnic table. I'll open this. I haven't told Trixie."

"I suppose I should. He's not going away. I just wish there was something I could do."

Haley went out back and found Mabel, Trixie, Sam and Sheriff Allen sitting at the table. There was already a bottle of wine open.

"Hello Haley," said the Sheriff. He was drinking a glass of wine, as was Sam. Did that mean he wasn't working.

"Hello," she said.

Sam nodded at her smiling.

"How are things at the Jensens? she asked Sam.

"Things are good. They found a place in the bunkhouse for me. I wanted to be close to the horses. I've still got a couple mares who haven't foaled yet. But neither of them are going to do it tonight, so I thought I'd drive into town and see how everybody's doing."

"How do you know they won't foal tonight?" asked Trixie.

"Their udders and teats don't look right. They swell up at night, but contract up during the day. When a mare's getting close, the udder fills with milk and stays swollen. There are other signs, but those are the first ones."

Trixie nodded. "I want to raise horses when I grow up. I love horses," she said, a dreamy look on her face.

Her daughter was still so young.

"You never did say what brings you here, Sheriff," said Mom.

"Just paperwork. Mabel's selling a lot of cars and I just wanted to make sure all the T's were crossed and the i's dotted."

"I didn't know you got involved with selling cars," said Haley. That puzzled her.

"Oh you know, that *Granny Bandit*, they got a make on a couple of the vehicles used and they're close to the type Mabel's selling, so I just needed to check them out. Because we know our Mabel's not the bandit." He smiled at Mabel.

Haley stared at Mabel while she dished up some steak and corn on the cob. The steak smelled incredible. It was juicy and there was still a little pink in it. She sliced a bite off and put it in her mouth, savoring the beefy flavor mingled with smokiness from the charcoal. She closed her eyes in bliss.

Then it hit her that Mom had said Mabel had come into some money lately. Something about a dead relative. She watched Mabel who was busy pouring wine for people. Mabel was a very interesting woman.

She didn't look in her seventies and she didn't act like it either. She kept herself fit and her mind was sharp. Haley wouldn't put it past Mabel to be the *Granny Bandit*, except that Mabel had been such a stickler for honesty in Elementary School. And Mabel had always been uncompromising. Perhaps she'd changed.

Mabel remained an enigma.

MABEL SPENT THE NEXT TWO DAYS ENTERTAINING HER GUESTS and volunteering at the gym.

The gym was packed with people and smelled of too many unwashed bodies. But the children needed entertainment, so she went to help out.

There was a jar set on the volunteer table for donations to help people out. If federal or state money came, it would be a while. Every day Mabel dropped in a few hundred dollars when no one was watching.

On the third day, Sheriff Allen came to take Bea, Haley and Trixie out to Bea's house. He wouldn't let them go alone. People weren't allowed to leave the highway and drive into evacuated areas.

Sam decided to follow them in his car and invited Mabel to come along. He wanted to check on his property as well.

Mabel dressed in old baggy jeans and work boots. It might be muddy. She wore a yellow t-shirt with a blue windbreaker on top.

She climbed into Sam's pickup, which smelled of roses. He had a sachet dangling from the mirror. Not many men would have flowers in their cars. Too worried about their masculinity. No wonder she liked him.

Mabel had wanted to go and see how high the river was, but hadn't really want to spend any more time with the Sheriff than she had to. It wouldn't do for him to get suspicious of her.

Mabel sipped on a bottle of water she'd brought. Silly to bring a bottle of water to go see a flooding river, but she knew she'd get thirsty. She sure hoped Bea's house was okay.

Sam followed the sheriff's Jeep off the highway onto Bea's road and both of them turned the vehicles around, so they could leave quickly if necessary. Good thing Bea had a wide road.

Mabel could see the Blackfoot. That wasn't good. The Sheriff stopped his Jeep close to the highway. Obviously, they were going to walk in, not drive. Everyone got out.

Still, Sam parked off to the edge and Mabel had to sidle next to his truck when getting out, trying to avoid the stickery wild roses and other bushes until she got past and could walk in the middle of the gravel road.

They walked a ways until they came to where the gravel road turned into a gravel parking lot. There was the driveway, some of the parking lot and then the river.

Bea's house was gone. Mabel couldn't even see the foundation. It was all underwater or maybe totally gone. The water was murky and churning too much to tell.

Mabel looked at Bea. She had that hardened look on her face. The same look she had when talking about how a cow or horse had died. It was like a protective shell, that wouldn't let the world see how much she was hurting. How she wouldn't let herself acknowledge how much she hurt. Not till she was alone, at least.

Haley looked shocked. Mabel realized she'd lost her childhood home. And her newest home, too.

Trixie's face was all wrinkled up as if she was ready to cry, but holding it back. She came from a long line of people who held back their emotions. Mabel went to Trixie and put her arm around the girl's shoulder and her crutches.

The river was loud. Mabel almost had to shout to be heard above it.

"Don't worry honey. Bea will rebuild. Then you'll have an all new home to live in."

"It won't be the same."

"No. It won't. But it will be better. You'll see."

Trixie smiled at her hopefully.

Sheriff Allen said, "Well that's a shame. A damn shame."

They stood about thirty feet from the river. Mabel could feel the spray from the water. She could see the far bank. The Blackfoot was ten times the normal width. She didn't have an eye for measuring but it must have been at least a mile wide.

The entire forest in the span of the current had been cut down by the river. Carried away.

The current carried downed trees and buildings from upstream. Muddy water churning. Strange shapes bobbed to the top, were taken under and then reappeared again farther downstream.

All she could smell was water carrying churned up soil and trees. There was a freshness, but a violence to it.

A dark form moved past her. She saw him. That man. Haley's ex.

"Hey you!" she yelled. Where had he come from?

She looked behind. Saw his car pulled over up the gravel road, just this side of Sam and the sheriff's vehicles. He must have followed them from town.

He walked up to Haley, stood in front of her and tapped her on the shoulder.

Haley yelled, probably to be heard above the river, "What are you doing here?"

"I have to talk to you. You keep avoiding me."

"I have nothing to say to you."

"I'm willing to share custody. Be reasonable."

"I don't trust you."

"I've changed," he said.

He was standing in front of Haley, his back towards the river.

Trixie moved closer to Mabel. She put both her arms around the girl. The man never once looked at Trixie.

The river seemed to be rising higher.

Mabel moved Trixie farther back from the river. Sam pulled Bea back as well.

"I deserve a chance to be a father."

"You had chances. For years. You drank your way through it."

"I don't drink as much any more. I could be good for you. We were perfect together."

Mabel knew that nothing Haley could say would convince him otherwise.

"Leave me alone." Haley gestured wildly. Pushing him away.

Sheriff Allen turned upstream.

He roared, "Everybody back!"

A huge clump of pines from upstream had been taken by the Blackfoot. Several two hundred foot tall trees whirled in the river's currents. They whacked other trees while moving through the water.

Haley must have seen it coming. She turned to run farther from the river.

The man said, "I will never leave you alone. Ever."

Then he was caught by one of the huge tree trunks. Swept beneath the surface of the river, as if he'd never been.

Mabel's mouth fell open.

Bea said, "Well, I'll be. ..."

Haley said nothing. She just stared, as if unbelieving.

They all stood for a long time. Watching the river.

No one spoke. They were all stunned into silence.

Finally, they were forced to leave. The Blackfoot kept growing in width.

Mabel helped Trixie past the man's car and into the sheriff's SUV, holding her crutches and putting them in afterwards. Then she went to Sam's truck and hauled herself up into the seat.

Sam drove out to the highway and headed back towards Lincoln. The drive back to town was silent. She and Sam didn't have anything to say.

Back home, she brewed some coffee and pulled out an old bottle of whiskey. She set glasses and cups on the counter. She pulled half-and-half and milk from the fridge, setting them out, along with a bowl of sugar. She put plates on the dining room table and some blueberry and apple muffins she'd gotten from Winnie's earlier in the morning. Then got a stack of paper napkins too.

Sam sat at the table, nervously tapping his fingers on the wood. When Bea, Haley, Trixie and Sheriff Allen got there, they filed in silently.

"There's coffee in the kitchen. You can make it however you like," Mabel said. She poured herself some coffee with a swig of whiskey in it and sat down at the dining room table. Glad she still had the vase of yellow daffodils on it. A promise of spring and hope.

They helped themselves to beverages and joined her at the table. No one spoke for a long time.

Finally, the Sheriff said, "I'll file a death certificate and make sure the car's towed away."

Haley nodded.

"When's the river supposed to crest?" asked Bea, after a long silence.

"Today, possibly tomorrow," said the Sheriff. "The bulk of the snow's melted and the weather forecasts are for clear skies.

No more rain to add to the mix. Hopefully, the river will go down quickly.

"Oh Sam, we didn't make it out to your place," said Bea.

"It's okay. I think I'll wait till the river's gone down a bit. I've seen enough of it for a while."

The Sheriff said, "Nothing you can do about anything until the water goes down, anyway."

Sam nodded.

"I'd better get back and check on my mares. Their colostrum's come in. They could foal anytime now."

"You worried about them?" asked Bea.

"No. I think they'll both do fine. Vet thinks so too. But it's they're first time. Just like to be around in case there's a problem," he said.

The Sheriff said, "I'd better get going too. Lots of things to keep track of. Thanks for the coffee and muffin." He stood, took one of the blueberry muffins, finished his coffee, set the mug on her counter and left.

Sam stood and took one of the apple muffins, almost as an afterthought. Haley walked him to the door.

"I'll be by in a day or so. See how you all are doing," he said. "Are you okay?"

"I'm okay. Just shocked," Haley said.

"Well, now you're free. No more hiding."

"No more hiding." Haley smiled, as if she'd just realized it.

Sam looked as if he wanted to say something else, but then stopped and went through the door.

Mabel looked at Bea. She was sipping her coffee, looking far away.

"What are you thinking about?" asked Mabel.

"I've got a lot of planning to do. Need to see how fast I can get a house built. One meant for running a B and B in. With larger rooms for those of us living there, including you Mabel.

And a more functional kitchen. And get fencing up, so I can move the livestock back."

"You'll need to get that insurance claim in as soon as you see all of the damage," said Mabel.

"Good thing I brought all my paperwork with me," said Bea. "I can get started."

Haley came back and plopped down in her chair.

Mabel looked around the table. Only Trixie looked sad.

"How are you doing?" Mabel asked her.

"I miss Twinkletoes and Trouble and the chicks." Mabel noticed she was hugging the stuffed animal she'd given her at the hospital.

"Maybe we can drive out and see them tomorrow," said Haley.

"You want to go down to the high school gym with me this afternoon?" asked Mabel. "I think we'll paint again. There's a few kids your age."

"Nice kids? Not bullies?"

"There will be no bullying while I'm around. Or when the other teachers are around either. We have no tolerance for bullying. Never have had."

Trixie nodded. "I think I'd like to go. If I'm going to go to school in Lincoln, I'd like to make some friend here."

"Good. I'll leave around one and I'll drive this time."

Life was looking up. Mabel was getting a new home. And a family.

It would be nice to have family again.

CHAPTER 29 ~ HALEY

Haley stood leaning on the rail fence at one of
Jensen's pastures, rubbing Sooty's ears. The gelding stretched
his head out sideways, eyes closed and lower lip quivering in
pleasure. She rubbed gobs of fur off his neck.

"About time you're getting rid of that coat. Summer will be
coming soon. Time to shed out."

She could see white, brown and black spots in the pasture
where various horses had been rolling and losing fur. It was a
brilliant spring day. The sun shone down and the weather was
so warm Haley just wore a blue t-shirt, jeans and boots. Not
even a hoody.

The air smelled of horse and cow manure. Smelled like a
ranch. Smelled like home.

Trixie sat behind her on a big rock, petting Trouble. The
dog had missed her terribly.

Twink hadn't been quite as lonely. She'd allowed herself to
be worshipped by Trixie, sleeping in the sun on a window seat
in a bay window in the house. Then she fell asleep.

They'd stayed inside for a while, drinking coffee and eating buttery chocolate chip cookies that Sarah Jensen had made. Then Bea had gone outside to play with her baby chickens.

Apparently, after she'd packed up and left the house for the last time, Sam, Dani and Jerry had brought friends, with several big trucks, opened the house with a spare key Bea had given Sam. They'd loaded up all of Bea's antique furniture, from the house and all the cabins. They had a flatbed as well, and put her homemade chicken coop on it, hauling it over to Jensen's. Her furniture was taken to one of the friend's barn for storage until the flooding ended.

Bea was ecstatic that she still had the chicken coop she'd built. She'd burst into tears when she first saw it had been saved.

Sam was working with the two new fillies who'd been born. Getting them used to being handled. Trixie had wanted to help, but with the crutches, he wouldn't let her into the paddock. The mares were first time moms and a bit nervous. A few more weeks and Trixie would be free of her crutches.

Haley smiled at her daughter. She was glowing. Trixie finally felt safe. It had helped for her to go to the high school gym with Mabel.

She'd made friends with another girl, Sian. They both loved animals and the same books. She'd come over to Mabel's yesterday. Haley had met her parents and they were relieved their shy daughter had found a friend.

Haley heard a meow and looked over to see Trixie petting a scrawny looking kitten who seemed desperate for attention. A beautiful orange tabby with a white belly and feet.

Sam walked up and leaned against the fence near her.

"Is that the Jensen's kitten?"

"They don't have a kitten. Sarah said this one's been hanging around for a day or so. I'd guess its home got washed away. Looks like it could use a meal."

"I should ask Sarah if they can feed it some of Twink's food."

"You could take a photo and put up a poster at the gym. See if anyone claims it. I'd guess if no one does, then it has a home," he nodded at Trixie, who was holding the kitten in her arms. Trouble was licking the cat.

"Don't know what Twink's gonna think about that."

"She'll adjust. I think she's a pretty adaptable cat," said Sam.

Haley nodded.

She'd be glad when the river retreated far enough to get started building Mom's new house. She missed the ranch. Missed the forest and nature. Mabel's tiny back yard wasn't enough.

Sam said, "So. If I cleaned up and picked you up at four, do you think there's a chance I could take you out on that date we missed."

She raised her eyebrows. She'd almost forgotten that date. So much had happened in the meantime. Everyone's life was in flux. When Haley did remember, she'd assumed he forgot. What with his mares giving birth.

"I think that would be lovely. I don't think they'll miss me at all."

"Good. Shall we drive to Missoula for dinner?"

"Yes. Let's."

"Good. Dancing afterwards? Or a movie?"

"Can we decide after dinner?" she asked.

"Sure."

"Okay, well I'd better go round up Mom. We need to get back to Mabel's. I'll need to clean up."

He nodded and said, "See you at four." Then headed off towards the bunkhouse.

"Mom, look at this cutie. Can I bring her back to Mabel's with us? She doesn't have a collar. I don't think she belongs to anyone."

Haley sighed. Mom appeared behind her.

"What do you think?" asked Haley. "Would Mabel mind?"

Mom said, "I doubt it. She likes cats. We'd need to get a litter box and food."

Haley said, "Okay, but we have to put up a flyer in the gym. See if she belongs to someone. And if she doesn't we need to take her to the vet, make sure she's healthy and neutered. You sure it's a she? Orange females aren't that common."

"Mom, I know the difference between a girl and a boy cat. She's a girl."

"Okay, well give her to me. I don't think you can carry her and walk on crutches. She'll have to stay inside at Mabel's. Mabel's too close to the highway."

"Okay. We'll only be at Mabel's for a few more months, right?"

"Right."

Haley took the loudly purring orange kitten. The kitten opened her eyes and looked at Trixie warily, although kept up the noise.

"It's okay honey. We'll keep you safe."

The soft kitten curled up in her arms, settling in and purring louder.

Once Trixie was in the front seat of the car with her crutches, Haley handed her the kitten who nestled in with her.

Haley climbed in the driver's seat and Mom got in the back. They drove off back to town.

New dreams whirled around in Haley's mind. The future held hope.

help other readers find books they might love. A review can be as simple as telling someone what stuck with you from the book. Thank you so much!

ABOUT THE AUTHOR

Linda Jordan writes fascinating characters, visionary worlds, and imaginative fiction. She creates both long and short fiction, serious and silly. She believes in the power of healing and transformation, and many of her stories follow those themes.

In a previous lifetime, Linda coordinated the Clarion West Writers' Workshop as well as the Reading Series. She spent four years as Chair of the Board of Directors during Clarion West's formative period. She's also worked as a travel agent, a baker, and a pond plant/fish sales person, you know, the sort of things one does as a writer.

Currently, she's the Programming Director for the Writers Cooperative of the Pacific Northwest.

Linda now lives in the rainy wilds of Washington state with her husband, daughter, four cats, a cluster of Koi and an infinite number of slugs and snails.

Her other work includes:
-*Horticultural Homicide: A Gina Wetherby Mystery*
-*Poison Passion: A Gina Wetherby Mystery*
-*Living in the Lower Chakras*
-*Notes on the Moon People*
-*Faerie Unraveled: The Bones of the Earth, Book 1*
All her work can be found at your favorite online bookseller.

Get a FREE ebook!
Sign up for Linda's Serendipitous Newsletter at her website:
www.LindaJordan.net
She can be found on Facebook at:
www.facebook.com/LindaJordanWriter
Metamorphosis Press website is at:
www.MetamorphosisPress.com
Goodreads: https://www.goodreads.com/author/show/
2021274.Linda_Jordan

Writers love reviews, even short, simple ones and honest
reviews help other readers find the book. Please go to where
you bought this book, or Goodreads, and leave a review. It
would be much appreciated.